WANTED: POT BELLIED PIGS

To Arica,

Pig Out On Books!

Colleen Copeland
1993

WANTED:
POT BELLIED PIGS

Written By
COLENE COPELAND

Cover and Illustrations

Sheila Somerville

JORDAN VALLEY HERITAGE HOUSE

WANTED: POT BELLIED PIGS

Copyright 1993, by Colene Copeland

Manufactured in the U.S.A.

Library of Congress Catalog Card number: 93-078897

ISBN: 0-939810-15-8 (Hardback)
ISBN: 0-939810-16-6 (Paperback)

First Edition

My thanks to:

Dr. Michael Meiners, our friend and veterinarian, who not only takes care of our "for real" animals, but advises me on the care and treatment of the little critters in my stories.

And to Diane Waggerby and her partner, Marianne Roley-Huber of Hubbard, Oregon for their friendship and up-to-date expertise shared with us on the subject of Pot Bellied pigs. No where in the northwest could you find better breeders of pigs for pets than these women. Gentle hands and know-how turn baby pigs into loving pets and champions.

And to my family who always pitch in to help with the work when I am busy writing a new book.

Dedication
To my mom and dad
for teaching me good values
and how to make work fun.

CONTENTS

Chapter 1.

NABBED

Hello! My true name is Lucy Lo Chow. I am a Vietnamese Pot Bellied pig. In the past few years popularity for pigs like me has taken a transonic leap. Half the folks in the U.S.A. want to own one of us for a pet. Half the rest are thinking about it.

Some of us live uptown, ride in limousines, wear spiffy fur coats and diamond necklaces. And we eat so well our bellies drag. I mean, *really drag*, ---more than normal.

Then there are pigs like me who fall into a batch of rotten luck, finding ourselves knee deep in slime, without even stinking ditch water to wash us clean. We are starved and left without water. We get slapped around, kicked and battered. And cussed at. But the worst of it is, we become unwanted and unloved. And that hurts.

Right from the beginning I was mixed up in nothing but trouble. Because of my misfortune, Mama and Papa said I should be the one to tell the story. Now, Mama and Papa are not my real parents. You know who they are. They own the hog farm near Thomas Creek. Priscilla, a pet pig of theirs, took to calling them "Mama and Papa" years ago. So now, everybody does.

Some of the story I'm about to tell you is from my memory. The rest has been recalled and shared with me by my family and friends.

I'll begin the telling where I think it should begin, on one of the worst days of my entire life. The dog catcher had nabbed me and I was locked up.

There I stood looking down at the dismal, old cement floor of the County Humane Society. Outside, it was a beautiful spring day, for those fortunate enough to be out. As for me, my days in the sunshine were over. My doom was as sure as guts in a gopher. Why? Because the Humane Society has rules. Now, rules are necessary for the Society to function properly, but those necessary rules had spelled my fate.

It was the afternoon of the fourth day of my first time there. Time was running out for me. The way I had it figured I had only a few hours left to live, tops, if ol' Flo didn't get down here to claim me. Fat chance. She would never do it.

For about 99.9% of us who have the raw deal of

ending up here, a sudden ending awaits.

Unwanted pets. That's what they call us, unwanted. I tried not to think about it. When I did I felt sad and I cried. I just couldn't help it.

The people who work here are nice enough, but they don't realize some of us understand their language. They talk right in front of us. I wished they wouldn't. I understand almost every word. After all, I was raised around humans, not pigs! Since the day of my birth, when my feet touched the ground and I sucked in that first breath of clean, fresh Oregon air.

The rules of the Humane Society were painfully etched in my brain. When someone comes in looking for their lost pet they get a real shocker. Sometimes they arrive too late.

The Society rules clearly stated, "Dogs and cats not wearing collars and not claimed by their owners in three days are put down by 'lethel injection'." Sad news for many pet owners. But, if the animal is wearing a collar, it has five days to be claimed.

Luckily, I was wearing a black harness. Boy! A two day stay of execution.

I had heard the rules repeated again and again, all day long, for four days.

But what about us Pot Bellied pigs? Nobody said. We were new to the shelter. I'd seen dozens of dogs and car loads of cats, but only a pig now and then. We weren't mentioned in the rules.

Time was running out for Lucy.

My only friend was Pamela, one of the technicians. I was sure she liked me. Once in a while she stopped by and talked kindly to me. But when I answered, she didn't understand. I was quite surprised when she shared a big, delicious, red apple with me.

The people who worked there were always busy. Our feed arrived on time, our drinking water was clean and fresh and our floors were hosed and brushed often. I could tell by watching and listening to them, they all loved animals.

But I asked myself a million times, "What about Pot Bellied pigs?" Maybe I was better off not knowing. Were we on the same three day and five day ruling as dogs and cats?

When I was dumped into this place, I was placed in a pen with Duffy, a two month old Pot Bellied male. I was older, by one whole month, but he was heavier by about five pounds. I weigh twelve pounds and I'm short.

Strangely enough, Duffy wasn't greatly overjoyed when he was claimed the following morning. Could anything at home be worse than the fate awaiting him here? I didn't think so. Before we had a chance to get acquainted his family showed up, whether he liked it or not.

Now you've probably asked yourself how an intelligent pig like I am ended up in this place. I'm not saying this is a bad place. But is it necessary? Sad to say, yes, it is.

When you are in our position, lost or unwanted, this place is frightening. Every minute brings a hollow, hopeless feeling. My poor stomach ached and quivered, quivered and ached. And my head, my poor tortured head. I had constant, painful throbs from the unceasing barking of the dogs.

I was here because nobody ever told me about dog catchers! No one ever told me to stay in the house or in the yard! No one! Not even Flo Fevers, my owner.

Flo just had to own a Pot Bellied pig. Why? Because Flo is a fad-happy airhead. If hair spray is popular and the "in" thing to do, Flo sprays. If red lips are in, Flo paints her's red! When mini-skirts were the rage, Flo was the first to show off her bony legs. Now, mini-skirts are out and mini-pigs are in. Flo weighed anchor and plunged right in.

Floyd, Flo's husband, begged her not to get a pig.

"Pigs are different. You haven't got a gnat of a notion how to raise one."

Flo never listened to Floyd. She should have. A genius, Floyd is not. However, he does have a cool head and a little common sense.

Wanting to be the first in her neighborhood to own a pig for a pet, Flo hurried out and bought me. I became Flo's prized possession, something to show off to the neighbors. Never did she treat me like a pet, someone to play with and feel kindly toward. I became a new charm on her bracelet of social status.

How different things were now. Flo's little charm stood locked up in the animal shelter.

It made no sense to me why a dog catcher would hijack a Pot Bellied pig!

"I doubt if Flo brags on me now!" I thought to myself.

The very first time I tried to cross the street I got smacked with a double whammy! This little, white barking truck came cruising ever so slowly, down Bodger Avenue. I hurried across the street, then stopped and looked back at it from the curb. How was I to know it was the wrong thing to do? I'm just a little pig.

The goofy driver stopped right in the center of our street, as though he owned it. Lazily, he slipped out of the cab and poked along toward me. With that blissful look on his face, I thought he was just being friendly. But he tricked me. As quick as the strike of a snake he snatched me by a leg.

With a little warning I might have outrun this grinning, long legged, son of a pig pincher.

What a cruel, coldhearted trick to play on a little pig so unaccustomed to the devious ways of the world.

I squealed louder and wilder than I had ever squealed before. But no one came to my rescue. Not

He snatched me by a hind leg.
How humiliating!

even Flo. How foolish of me to think Flo cared enough to come to my rescue.

Being carried by a hind leg was uncomfortable as well as humiliating.

This grinning, idiot dog "shoh-fur" threw me in the back of his truck with a Great Dane who smelled awful, like a dog, and a small white shivering poodle. The shivering told me she was as frightened as I was. Neither of the dogs spoke to me on the way to the County Humane Society. Two more stops added four full grown cats and seven brown and white mongrel puppies.

For the first time in my life, I had something in common with dogs and cats. We were all scared to death. What would become of us?

Chapter 2.

A NEW FRIEND AND SADNESS

Four days had passed. I'd been left alone here to wonder and worry. There had been no sign of Flo or Floyd.

Rescuers arrived the afternoon of the first day for the Great Dane. His owners gave him a good tongue lashing. This was not the first time he'd run off.

"Last time," his owner said, "he fell into a tar pit and was stuck there for several hours." It had taken days to clean the dog. They'd practically skinned him alive in the process. "Thought he'd think twice before running off again, but he didn't!" the owner laughed.

I felt sorry for the hairless dog. He was so ugly. Before I heard about the tar pit I just figured all Great Danes looked that way. I tried not to laugh, even though it was great to have something to laugh about.

A very happy little girl in a blue and white striped

10

dress and a pony tail bailed out the poodle on the morning of the second day. The dog was still shivering. But these shivers were more of a happy nature. Loving arms lifted the thankful pet from the holding pen.

"Oh my Elizabeth," the little girl said joyfully, "I missed you so much! Are you all right? Are you hungry, my darling girl? Where you warm enough last night? It was lonely without you on my pillow." All the while the grateful pet hugged the girl's neck and licked her face.

Oh, to be loved like that! How wonderful it must feel! Flo bragged on me, but she never, ever loved me. To tell you the truth, I'm not too sure she even liked me.

One day Flo was talking to our neighbor, Alice Bennington. Flo was acting highfaluting. You know, like she was the chief "stuck-up know-it-all" on the block.

"You must get one, Alice. Pot Bellied pigs are in; the latest thing in house pets."

Alice was not impressed.

Flo did not let up. It was her way of saying, "Look at me. I have something that you don't, so that makes me superior."

"My Lucy is ever so smart and the cleanest pet I've ever owned."

Well, at least she got that part right. Flo boasted

how she'd paid $500.00 for me. Big deal! My mother cost $2000.00, but that was before the price of Pot Bellied pigs took a big drop.

"If Flo thinks I'm worth 'big money', then why doesn't she treat me better?" I wondered. She fed me dog food. Once in a while she threw me a bone. Pigs don't eat bones. Dogs eat bones.

Floyd was no better. Sometimes, he gave me cat food.

Now, I'm not stupid. It was either eat the stuff or go hungry. So, I ate it. But I can tell you one thing, that stuff was not fit for pig consumption. Always, I would protest, hoping one day one of them might get the message.

I would say to them, "Haven't you noticed, I don't bark! And I don't have fleas. I definitely do not meow, hiss, show teeth or kill mice!"

Food on their table smelled great. I often asked for fruit and vegetables, or pasta. I love pasta. And bread, my, I do love bread. But nary a crumb came my way. They paid less attention to my pleadings than they'd pay to a moldy melon in the garbage.

The dog and cat had no complaints. Their daily diet was perfect to the taste. To their taste, but not to mine.

Over and over I told them. "My stomach requires pig food. Don't you understand? The other stuff you feed me is close kin to Gag and Vomit. I hate it. My stomach hates it. My dreams turn to nightmares when I'm choking down another mouthful. I wake up in cold sweats with a rotten taste in my mouth." But nobody listened.

A half-way intelligent person (that leaves Flo out) would have gotten some facts about raising a pig before buying one. She bought me from the Carlsons. Surely, they told Flo what to feed me. More than likely they did and she just didn't listen to them. Flo thinks she knows more about everything than anybody else!

I never heard my mother complain about her food. As a matter of fact, I remember those great little pellets made of grains. They were quite tasty.

I missed my mother.

Confusion reigned at Flo's. Something was always afoot. A couple of days before my departure, the old Bulldog, Gus, chased the neighbor's cat right through the porch screen door, leaving a humongous hole. In came the flies. In came the bees and Gail Snooky's chocolate-faced twins.

All this commotion was too much for Flo. She had a hissy.

Suddenly, those thoughts were replaced by kind words being spoken by someone approaching my pen.

"Little pig, what are we going to do with you?"

I looked up to see. A shelter worker spoke calmly to the sickly looking pig she held cradled in her arms.

Gently, she positioned the new guest just inside my gate. The new pig and I stared at each other.

Putting two unfamiliar pigs in the same pen could prove dangerous, but these good folks didn't know that. Lucky for them, I am not the fighting and biting type.

This pig was a black female, a shade taller than I. She limped as she walked. Confused and miserable, she began to weep. Just like me and everyone else in this place, she was scared.

"Don't be sad," I told her. But she could not hear me for the cussed barking.

To tune out the noise was impossible. Sounds burst forth in all shapes and sizes, loud and soft barks, bays, whines and whimpers, pitiful cries and howlings. Constant howling.

The mood of the shelter house changed immediately when an owner retrieved his pet. We all wished it were us. Though we were envious, every animal in the shelter was happy for the one being claimed. Afterwards, calm prevailed for a minute or two, but no longer; the din soon returned.

I moved closer to the new pig so she could hear me. "My name is Lucy," I said loudly.

"They call me Wrinkle; I don't like my name very much," she said pitifully. "I feel kinda sick."

"This place will do that to you," I told her.

There were a couple of things about Wrinkle that

caused me to wonder about her. She was bruised, badly bruised. Dried blood was caked on the inside and outside of her left ear. The sticky part of it was yucky and smelly.

"What happened to you?" I asked her.

I probably should not have asked her that question. Now, she really began to cry. And when she cried, I realized that she was in a lot of pain. Her body jerked and quivered.

"They don't want me anymore," Wrinkle sobbed, "None of them except Aaron. He wanted to keep me. It wasn't my fault. I couldn't help it."

I didn't understand. I wished I knew the right words to make her feel better.

"Aaron and his mother went away for the weekend to visit his mother's sister. They left me at home with Cory, Aaron's father. That was a big mistake. I got no food or water. Cory was out beer drinking with his buddies. Worst of all, not once in those two days did he put me out to go to the bathroom. I couldn't help what happened. I had to go real bad."

The pig cried and coughed. When she breathed she made a hoarse, wheezing sound. I felt sorry for her. She was really sick.

"Last night," she continued, "after dark, Cory brought me over here and tied me to a tree in the parking lot."

Wrinkle fell to her side and coughed even harder.

Blood oozed from her nose and mouth.

"Cory wears pointed, steel toed boots. He kicked me as hard as he could, lots of times and called me a filthy pig," she cried. "I'm *not* a filthy pig!"

She was suffering so and I was completely helpless.

Now she lay motionless and bled more profusely, from the mouth. I squealed for help as loud as I could. I jumped on the gate and rattled it again and again. Finally, a busy worker heard my pleadings.

"What's the matter, Little Miss Pot Belly," he asked.

Quickly, I ran around Wrinkle several times, hoping to draw this fellow's attention to her. It worked. He came in and knelt down by Wrinkle.

"Oh my!" was all he said before racing down the cement walkway looking very worried. In a matter of seconds, he returned with help.

Wrinkle was dead.

"He kicked me real hard, lots of times," she had said. No doubt about it, this man Cory had kicked Wrinkle so hard, he'd caused her death.

How could anyone be so cruel?

Now it was my turn to cry. I cried myself to sleep wondering if I would be the next to die, unwanted and unloved.

Chapter 3.

PAM'S PLAN

Gail Snooky saw me carried off by Animal Control. She wasted no time in getting a-cross the street to tell Flo and Floyd. The twins bolted ahead of their mother, shouting the news, which annoyed Gail. She wanted to tell it. In no time at all everybody on the block had heard about my bad luck.

Flo reacted in a strange and peculiar manner. But then, how else would she react? Flo does everything strangely and peculiarly.

"I won't have that pig making me look foolish," she said, as if she needed any help with that. "I'll sell it. That's exactly what I'll do. The first person who offers me $750.00 can just go down there and claim her."

Floyd was amused. "How much? Where are you going to get a buyer and how much time do you

17

think you've got, for crying out loud?"

Common sense was as foreign to Flo as a green crocodile in a gray cookie jar.

"Whatever do you mean, Floyd, 'How much time have I got'? I've got as long as it takes!" she croaked.

"Wrong!" Floyd grinned. "If you don't go down to the shelter and claim that pig of yours, they'll put her to sleep, it doesn't matter how much she's worth, and you'll be out your $500.00 that you shouldn't have spent in the first place."

"Go call them," Floyd ordered. "And you'd better do it quick or you won't have a pig to talk about. In fact, she may be 'put down' already."

Flo was not about to take orders from Floyd. But this time, although it was hard for her to admit it, she figured just this once her husband might be right. Slowly, and at the same time darting defiant looks at Floyd, she looked up the number for the County Humane Society.

"My little Pot Bellied pig got out. I was wondering if by any chance she's there?" Flo asked, ever so sweetly.

"You know it is," Floyd said to her back. Flo growled and waved him off.

After a while Flo hung up the phone and stared out the kitchen window. It was a fixed stare, eyes wide open. Flo was scheming.

"Well?" Floyd inquired.

"They get pigs all the time. There is *one* there that got picked up off the street, ---a black and white female."

"Probably Lucy," Floyd told her.

Flo picked up her purse. "One of us has to go down there and claim her. I'll just go down there and tell them I'm trying to sell that run-away pig. They can keep it for a few days."

"Flo," Floyd gave his wife a disgusted look. "The Humane Society is not in the baby sitting business. They perform a great, thankless job for the community."

Floyd didn't know it, but he had started an argument. A loud and lasting argument! It wasn't Floyd's pet. Not for any amount of money would he go to the shelter to pick it up.

"That pig has made me look like a fool," Flo spouted.

"Not too hard a thing to do," Floyd snapped back.

The fight could be heard easily a block away. After about an hour they both cooled down and went out for a pizza. The fighting made them hungry.

Things did not look good for me. Floyd wouldn't lift a finger because I wasn't his. Flo had decided she wouldn't disgrace herself by picking up a pig who was dumb enough to get caught in the first place. So, that was that.

In the meantime the hard working, animal-loving folks at the Humane Society had a big problem. It was my fifth day to be in the shelter. Doomsday!

Each day, the staff held a meeting in the worker's lounge about twenty minutes before the doors opened to the public. The director asked if there were any urgent problems. If I had been there I would have yelled, "Yeah. Me!"

But I wasn't there. Fortunately, Pamela was. You know, the technician who had taken a liking to me.

"I can't bear to see that little black and white pig put to sleep. I know it's the fifth day and I know we are overcrowded, but this one is so special and fairly healthy. I have an idea that just might save her. Some friends of my family live on a small farm near Thomas Creek. Nobody knows more about hogs than this couple. I'm pretty sure I can get them to pick up at least one of these orphan pigs and care for it until a suitable home can be found. If you'll give me another day or two, I'd like to try. In fact, if it's all right with the rest of you, I'll call them this morning."

"Pam, that sounds wonderful, almost too good to be true!" Mrs. Bates, the director, responded. "To know we had that kind of help with these Pot Bellies would be short of a miracle. Who would ever dream we would have pigs in the shelter? We are not equipped for them. I have a feeling as their popularity grows we will see more and more of them ending up here. It's sad. Pet owners mean well; they see these cute little fellows and have to have one. Biggest majority of the owners know very little about the habits of a pig or how to properly care for and feed one." She smiled at Pam. "Yes, Pamela, by all means. Call your friends. We'll put a hold on this pig until you have had a chance to talk to them about it."

I had no idea what was going on. They didn't *think* to tell me. Everytime a worker came near my pen I thought my time was up.

Pam was thankful for a chance to help me. "This pig is special. She's so unhappy. I'd swear she knows and understands the way the shelter works. She brightens up when another pig comes in. As soon as it is gone she seems sad again."

"And how about her yelling for help when that injured pig needed it?" someone mentioned. "And then the poor pig died, right in front of her."

The director reported that a cruelty investigation was pending on that particular pet owner. The pig had been found tied to a tree in front of the Humane Society, just like Wrinkle said. There were multiple bruises to its head and body and two fractured legs.

"I'm convinced! Someone kicked that poor little thing in the head so hard and so many times it caused it's death," she told them. "Oh, I hope we find the wacko who did this."

Mrs. Bates was a real scrapper. She was dedicated

to the protection of animals and could be a real she-devil when one had been abused, like this one. In this case the animal had been beaten to death. Mrs. Bates was irate! God help this man Cory if she caught up with him.

All they had to do was ask me! I knew who did it and I'd be glad to tell on him. Wouldn't you?

As soon as the meeting broke up, Pam headed for the telephone. She hoped with all her heart her friends could help her.

But would it be soon enough to save me? She would just have to try.

Chapter 4.

PAPA AND MAMA

Pamela's friends on the farm were none other than the pig farmers you have come to know as Papa and Mama.

Life is much more simple for them now. A few years ago their farrowing barn was filled to capacity. I've been told that fifty to sixty sows at one time was not a bit unusual. The work load was heavy then and the days lasted long into the night. The sows almost always gave birth to their babies at night when the barn was quiet. Papa and Mama never failed to be on hand when the sows farrowed. That means, when the babies were being born.

Priscilla was born way back then. She was a little runt pig, raised in the house. The family still talks about her even though she has been dead and buried on the farm for many years.

Today, the giant barns look a little lonely. Often,

23

Mama and Papa walk through them, reminiscing. They tell wonderful stories. Some are sad, some are funny, but they love remembering and I love hearing about all of it.

Only eight sows and one boar remain. Pets and favorites, every one. Little Prissy, Priscilla's daughter, is getting along in years. When she's in the farrowing barn she still occupies the same pen as always, so I'm told. So do her daughters, Penny and Patsy, sisters from the same litter and grown sows now. Then there is Pee Dee from another of Prissy's litters. Across the hall from Patsy you'll find Starlight, Patsy's daughter. She's the one they say is a dead-ringer of Mabel, Priscilla's mother. The other three sows are descendants of Hotsie, Papa's prize Chester White sow who died just before Priscilla.

Most of the work in the farrowing barn has been turned over to Arley Willett and his family. Everybody who knows Papa says it's a wonder he trusted his hogs to anyone, he's so particular.

The Willetts are a hard working, kind and gentle Mennonite family. Arley had worked for Papa, off and on, for several years before he took full responsibility for the barns. When Arley is needed in the fields on his own farm, any member of his family can fill in at the barns. He has a wife, Ellen, and four sons ranging in age from nine to fifteen years.

Does that mean that Papa and Mama stay out of

An M&M candy for Starlight.

the barns? Perish the thought! The hogs are part of the family. Talking to them every day and lavishing them with special treats is a part of their daily life. By the time Papa walks through the orchard located between the farm house and the barns, his pockets are bulging with apples, when they are in season, Winesaps, Jonathans and Golden Delicious. Mama is just as bad. She wears an apron with special made pockets. On her way through the garden she loads up those pockets with whatever is available. She likes to bring watermelon size zucchini. One is enough. She puts it on a feed barrel and cuts a few cubes for everybody.

The barn cats jump up to check it out. One sniff and they are gone. A chunk of meat is more to their liking.

Even though Dr. Mike tells Mama to stop giving Starlight M&M candies, she does it anyway. She finally agreed to give her just one. But what she didn't tell him was, she really meant one package.

"She loves them so much," she told Papa. "One little package can't hurt that big sow."

And as usual, Mama carries on a daily conversation with Little Prissy. Papa thinks it a bit bazaar, but it's a fact and one that has come in helpful over the years, so I've heard.

Actually each day was quite a bit like the other and once in a while, a little lonely. Until the day of Pamela's phone call. No one suspected then what that one phone call would lead to.

Mama and Papa had known Pamela all her life. In the fall she planned to attend a school of Veterinary Medicine.

"That little girl will make a great vet," I heard Papa say, "the way she loves animals."

With all the unwanted animals Pamela saw every day, I always wondered why she took a special liking to me.

Her call was a plea for help. A tear rolled down her cheek and splattered on her arm as she dialed the number.

"You guys, we are desperate!" she had said. "This one little Pot Bellied pig is so special. Her time in the shelter has expired. No one has claimed her. You know what happens to unclaimed animals here. We don't have room enough to keep them all. Just a few ever get adopted. Please talk it over. See if you can possibly take just this one."

Mama sensed Pamela's desperation. She told her she would talk it over with Papa and let her know in the morning. Then, she went one step further.

"We will be there at 9:30 in the morning to see the pig." She hung up the phone on the kitchen wall and turned to Papa.

"What a tender-hearted, animal-loving girl Pamela is. You are right about her. She will make a great veterinarian one day." Mama stood there a minute with her hands rammed down in her apron pockets, thinking. "Papa, she called to ask a favor. I can't remember her ever doing that before."

Papa was always willing to lend a hand. "A favor? Something we can help with?"

Mama laughed. "That depends! What do you know about Vietnamese Pot Bellied pigs?"

"More than you think, probably," Papa grinned. "They used to run wild. They ate and slept out in the jungles. I read it somewhere. The pigs moved around, following the food supply. They fed on whatever was in season, nuts, berries, grass and of course roots. I know when it was hot they stayed by water holes and in the winter they piled up in caves, ---slept and waited for better weather. I also know that a few years ago they were brought into this country for house pets. I was sure you'd want one, Mama. They sold for big bucks too, $5,000.00 to $10,000.00. But not anymore. Every time I go to a livestock auction, I see a few sell. Some of them look terrible, like they've been underfed. More often though, they look overfed."

"Well now! Papa, I'm impressed that you know so much about them. Well, I've heard about them too. And yes, I did think I might like one. The State Fair had a few pens of them. Boy, were they popular. Always a crowd around the pens and people asking questions of the owners. And, I've read several articles in the newspapers and magazines. A lot of it was about zoning, having to do with whether or not a pig could be kept in the city limits. Looks like to me if they are miniatures and are house pets they don't really fit into the farm hog catagory."

Finally, Papa became suspicious. "Why are we talking about Pot Bellied pigs? You said Pamela needed a favor. Has to do with pigs, huh?"

"Lately the Humane Society is having to contend with more and more Pot Bellied pigs. Pam's job there is good preparation for Veterinarian School."

"What does one thing have to do with the other?" Papa asked.

"Nothing, I guess. I just know Pam has gotten herself attached to a little Pot Bellied pig. One that was picked up by the Dog Catcher," she told him.

"A Dog Catcher?" Papa laughed.

"It is kinda funny. Probably not very funny to that poor little pig. Nobody has claimed it. Pamela is afraid it will have to be put down. In fact, today is its fifth day. Normally, it would have been destroyed by now, but Pam begged for its life. She said we are her only hope, Papa. If we don't take it, ---well, you know."

Papa picked up his binoculars and looked at some yellow birds in an apple tree. He too was thinking. No one loves animals, especially pigs, more than Mama and Papa.

"Where would we put it?" he asked.

"I don't really know. In the house I guess," Mama answered thoughtfully.

"When did you tell Pam we would let her know?"

"I told her we would be in at 9:30 in the morning to have a look at the pig. We'll tell her then, I guess, one way or the other."

Papa and Mama looked at each other for a long minute, still thinking.

"How about we take the day off? I know a few families who raise Pot Bellies. Let's go visiting." Papa began to grin. He was having a good time just thinking about it. Like a new adventure.

At first Mama wasn't sure. But Papa's excitement was contagious. She fell right in with it. While she took off her apron and fixed up a little, Papa made some phone calls. He sounded a little pushy on the phone.

"We are coming over," he told everybody he talked to. "Just wanted to be sure you still have Pot Bellied pigs."

By 10:30 a.m. they were half way to Albany. The first breeder on their route, Jean Miller, had four little sows. Little to Mama and Papa. These little sows wouldn't weigh more than fifty pounds if they were soaking wet.

Jean loved talking about pigs. But what she wanted more than anything else was a buyer. She admitted it was harder selling pigs for $200.00 than it had been a few years ago when the price was ten times that.

The pigs were in a barn. Mama thought that was strange. "How many of these pigs have been in the house?" Mama asked just out of curiousity.

The breeder hesitated. She seemed embarrassed about answering. Finally, when Mama and Papa both stared at her waiting for an answer, she said, "Just this sow." She pointed to a black sow nursing three, three week-old pigs.

"I don't mean to sound stupid, but how do you make house pets out of them if you raise them in the barn?" Mama asked.

Mrs. Miller changed the subject.

Papa asked questions about feed, weight of the pigs at various ages, etc. Mama asked about temperament and how long it takes to housebreak one. They both scratched a lot of ears and petted all of them.

They were surprised to learn that the weight of an adult sow can vary from 30 to 150 pounds. Under some conditions they become even larger.

The question about housebreaking went unanswered. Maybe this breeder just didn't know.

"We are trying to decide if we want to get a pig or not." Mama didn't tell her they had no intention of buying one from her.

Jean didn't know that. She handed them a couple of her business cards and told them if they had any questions to call her.

Papa and Mama both felt a little guilty for taking the woman's time. However, not sorry enough to stop them from visiting three more breeders before they stopped for a bit of lunch. Mama got into a friendly conversation with the waitress at the truck stop about Pot Bellied pigs. Waitresses hear everything. This waitress told them about two families in Albany who had pigs for pets.

All in all it was a very productive day for information. They both had taken lots of notes, each in his own way. One fellow loaned them some magazines about exotic animals. Pot Bellied pigs are considered exotic animals. Each issue had a pig section.

Mama and Papa had much to talk about at the supper table.

As for me, it was the eve of the sixth day. What kind angel, I wondered, had given me an extra day to live?

Pamela came by. She seemed so sad. But she stopped once and spoke directly to me.

"I'm trying, little pig, I'm trying," she walked on with a tear in her eye.

I had no idea what she meant. I was again left alone in the misery of the noise. What would tomorrow bring for me?

Chapter 5.

A LITTLE BIT OF LUCK

For a couple of minutes on the morning of my sixth day it was so quiet in the shelter, I heard a bird singing out in the puppy run.

"Only a beautiful bird could sing like that," I thought. I was sure I would never see a songbird again, or anything else outside these walls. Springtime and all the beauty of the season was just outside, so near and yet totally out of my reach.

The big yellow Labrador was taken to the adoption area this morning. Lucky fellow. He would stay there now until someone gave him a new home. I wondered why he was here.

I was given a good breakfast. Pig pellets! I could hardly believe it! They were delicious! They were the first I'd had since leaving my mother. Ben Edwards even gave me a piece of his donut. It was yummie!

I had been thinking it must be Pamela's day off.

33

Then I heard someone call for her to come to the office. I knew she had lots of work to do, but I hoped she would come by later to see me.

When the barking resumed it was the worst I had ever heard. It echoed through the building and bounced off the walls. My head felt as though it might crack wide open.

Suddenly, my gate opened. There stood Pam with a leash in her hand. She bent over me and attached it to my harness, the one Flo put on me so she could parade me up and down the street and brag about owning a pig.

"Good morning, little Pot Belly. How would you like to go for a walk? A couple of friends of mine are here to see you."

"Oh no! What is she really going to do with me? Where is she taking me?" I thought for sure my final hour had come.

I was forced to go along with her out of the barking room and into a quiet zone. My ears could not believe their good fortune. She led me out to a little sun porch. It was nice. The furniture was the color of the yellow Labrador. The walls were lined with animal pictures, dogs and cats, ---no pigs, and there sat two friendly looking people, smiling at me.

"Here she is," Pamela told them.

I didn't understand. It sure wasn't Flo and Floyd, but another couple.

"Well hello there," the friendly fellow said, then turned to Pamela and asked, "How old do you suppose she is?"

Pamela led me over to him. "We don't know for sure. None of us know much about these pigs. But we think she is about three months."

"Three months and seven days," I told Pam. But of course she didn't understand, people never do, at least not the ones I had known.

"You are close, Pamela," the lady winked at me as if she understood me and was letting me know she did. No. That wasn't possible.

The lady sat down on the floor near me. She scratched behind my ears with her fingers.

"You sweet little thing," she said to me, "Papa and I looked at lots of Pot Bellied pigs yesterday and we saw dozens of pictures of even more, but none of them had eyes as kind as yours or a nose as cute."

"Well, kind eyes and a cute nose won't keep you alive when you're in this place. Not many of us ever leave by the front door," I replied.

"How sad," she said, again as if she understood.

The fellow gave her an odd look, as if he didn't want her to talk to me.

"Pamela," he said, "Why don't you leave the three of us in here for a while, say half an hour."

"Sounds good to me," Pamela replied. "You guys get acquainted and I'll see ya later."

I saw no reason to fear these people.

"Mama, I didn't want to ask in front of Pam. Don't tell me you can understand this pig!"

Mama laughed. "What's so strange about that? A pig is a pig, I guess, This one sounds like a mini- Priscilla or Little Prissy."

"What's your name, honey?" she asked me.

"Flo called me Lucy. My mother didn't call me anything," I answered. Wait a minute! I was talking to a human and the human was talking back.

"Lucy? I would call you Lucy Lo Chow. You know why? Because you carry your chow, way down low," she laughed. "Everybody calls us Mama and Papa. We've never had a Pot Bellied pig on the farm, but we've raised hundreds of farm hogs over the years."

"Why are you here?" I asked.

"Pam wanted us to meet you," Mama told me.

I figured if Mama understood me then so did Papa. I was wrong.

"Have you folks always been able to communicate with pigs?" I asked Papa. That was a mistake.

He asked Mama for help. "What's she sayin'?"

I wondered why that was. But I didn't ask. Everytime I spoke, she translated.

"I think you are a pretty fine pig," Papa said to me. "And, I can see Mama likes you too. If you think you can put up with us, we will take you out to the farm to live with us. Pam says that nobody came to claim you. I can't imagine why. Until we can find you a proper kind of family to live with, you can make your home with us. O.K.?"

A big ol' lump came up in my throat. Look at me. Some good fortune, I'd say. I will never, ever forget Pamela for her kindness. Without her, I'd be dead.

"Yes, oh yes, I'd love to go home with you, Thank you for wanting me. I hope I won't be any bother." I cried.

Papa went to the office to fill out the necessary papers. Mama talked to me about the farm. After a while Papa returned.

"Guess what? While I was standing in the office some woman walked in with a pig in her arms. She practically threw it at the lady at the reception desk. Then she turned and took off in a huff, like she was mad as the dickens."

"How awful!" Mama was shocked. Wait until I tell her about Wrinkle.

Pamela came in wearing her long blue jacket and a great big grin. "I'm so glad you guys are taking little Pot Belly. I knew you'd hit it off."

"Her name is Lucy," Mama said.

"Oh, you've named her already?" Pam asked.

Papa looked at Mama. She started to say, "No, she told me her name is Lucy." But Papa poked her so she wouldn't say it. I guess he didn't want anyone to know that Mama can talk to pigs. Humans are strange.

"Did you bring something to put her in?" Pam asked.

"Heavens no, honey! She can ride in the front seat with us." Mama replied cheerfully.

"Wow! The front seat! Gosh, little Pot Belly, how about that?" Pam was happy for me.

She walked us to the car and waved goodbye as we drove away, with me right between them in the front seat. Before we had gone far, I laid my head on Mama's lap and she loved me up. My goodness, it was nice. I decided I was just about the luckiest pig in the world.

You might think because of my happiness the story ends here. Well, you'd better think again. We hadn't seen the last of Flo. She wanted her $500.00 back and she would do anything to get it. You would not believe how much pain and misery that woman can dish out. When she finds out where I am, what do you think she will do?

Chapter 6.

THE FARM

From the moment we arrived, I loved the farm. We headed straight for the house. I was to be a part of the family. Before we went inside Papa walked me up under a big pine tree in the back yard.

"This is a good place to go to the bathroom, Lucy. Just because I can't understand your language like Mama does, doesn't mean I don't know how to take care of a pig," Papa said.

Flo made me use a cat's litter box in the house. It was humiliating. She fed me cat food and gave me a litter box. I'm surprised she didn't call me puss.

I guess a litter box is the best solution for a pig who lives in an apartment, but only if someone isn't around to take it outside a few times a day. At night it isn't necessary.

The entire house was mine to explore. Although

Mama and Papa kept an eye on me for a while, until they knew I was trustworthy. I felt safe and welcome.

A small, shiny, metal bucket was filled with water and placed on the floor in the kitchen for me. Every time they snacked on something, I got a tiny bite.

"Until we find out what a Pot Bellied pig is supposed to eat to stay healthy, we won't take any chances with you, Lucy Lo Chow," Mama told me. "You won't get hungry though. I know pigs can have fruits and vegetables. They won't hurt anybody."

Papa found a phone number for one of the Pot Bellied pig associations in the exotic animal magazines. He phoned them and asked for the very latest information they had on the care and feed of Pot Bellies.

"I visited several breeders and pet owners yesterday and no two of them fed the same way." He told them. "Every one claimed they knew what they were doing. About 75% of the animals I saw had been overfed and only one breeder had ever wormed her pigs." Before he hung up the phone, he wrote down a couple of phone numbers. "Well, if that don't beat all," he said as he chunked the phone down.

"What's wrong?" Mama asked.

"Something's mighty wrong here. If raising Pot Bellied pigs for pets was my business, I'll bet I'd be better informed that that woman was! Do you know what she told me?" Papa was pretty aggravated. "She didn't really bother to answer my question. She waltzed all around it. 'Different breeders prefer different formulas', I think that's what she said." Papa laughed. "Now that is news to me. There are a lot of different companies who produce good hog feed, but the formulas don't vary all that much. What a hog requires for good health, is what it requires for good health. The same would hold true for miniature pigs, but the amount you feed, and the formula, would have to be different. With our big hogs we have a specific mix for each age and condition, you know, like starter for pigs, then grower, then a finisher. Special formulas for the gestating and lactating sows. But you can't feed miniature pigs on farm hog feed. The idea is to keep them healthy, but at the same time keep them small at every stage of their life. I'll check with a few grain companies. One of them ought to know. If not, I'll go over to the Ag College and talk to the fellows where Dr. England used to be. In the meantime, Mama, we'll feed this little thing like you said, but add a little grain. That will keep her happy."

I was hanging around under their chairs, listening. Papa was going to a lot of trouble to feed me the right stuff.

After a while I was invited to go for a walk around the farm. I wasn't even on a leash. Most well behaved pigs don't require one anyway, except maybe in a crowd or traffic.

When we got to the back porch, there were those cussed four steps. I'd handled them easily going up, but going down could be embarrassing as well as dangerous for me. I knew if I stepped down the first step, I'd tumble down the rest. I was not anxious to break my neck or make a fool of myself, my first day here. When I halted at the steps, Mama nearly fell over me.

"I hate going down," I told her. "These short legs I came with can be a real drag at times. I can go up, but I cannot go down."

Mama laughed. "Then we'll make you a slide. Stay right where you are. It won't take long."

Mama told Papa about my problem. I soon learned how quickly they get things done. Papa measured the area and went to find a board to fit. Mama fetched a length of scrap carpeting to cover it. Papa fitted the board securely to the right side of the stairs. In a matter of minutes it was ready to be tried.

"Come on down!" they invited.

With them watching, I became shy. But I *was* anxious to give it a try. The slide looked great. It was about a foot wide.

First, I felt of it with my right foot and then the left. Then both at the same time. The carpet was thick, but smooth. Cautiously, I started down, half walking, half sliding. When I reached the ground I asked myself, "Self, why didn't you slide all the way?

I flew up the stairs, took aim,
and slid all the way down.

You'd had a lot more fun." So, I flew up the stairs, took aim and slid down, all the way. I loved it. It was fast and fun.

Mama and Papa were laughing. They made me feel wonderful! If ol' Flo could see me now! Good food, good friends, and a good slide, just for me.

"It's too good to be true. This will not last," I told myself.

Speaking of Flo, along about now Flo was having second thoughts about me. While I was getting a grand tour of my new home, rattling around in all the barns and buildings, another rattling was taking place. The one in Flo's head. Flo was thinking. Now, isn't that a real revelation!

"I have made up my mind," she announced to Floyd.

The two of them had been working on old Gus's dog house. Floyd wanted to build a new one. A good coat of paint would do just fine, according to Flo. Floyd never understood his wife's moods. When it came to spending money on home improvements she was as tight as the hide on a hog's nose. But when it came to something she couldn't live without, a fad-dish something, she would empty poor Floyd's wallet as quickly as I can squash a stink bug.

The topic of conversation was paint for the dog house. Naturally, Floyd thought Flo had selected a color when she said "I have made up my mind", --not so! You had to listen carefully to know how Flo's "mind" worked.

"I'm going down there. I'm going to the shelter and get that pig!"

"Flo, what are you talking about? You don't have a pig down there to go get. We've been all through this."

"That's all you know. I'm going!" And she did. She grabbed her purse, got in the car and took off toward the Humane Society. She had a plan. She'd pretend to be interested in adopting an animal, so she could snoop. She had it all figured out. When and if she found me, she would give them a hard luck story and take me home with her.

Thinking about Flo in that Humane Society makes me laugh. She gets so upset about the least little thing. I wonder how she handled the barking?

The shelter had lots of visitors. The parking lot was nearly full. Most everbody was looking for a lost pet. A few were shopping for a pet to own. Flo was looking for the pig who had made her look bad. Me! What she was really looking for was a way to get her money back. She nosed around until she found a pen with a pig in it. It was the pen where I had spent a few terrifying days.

Remember the pig that was brought in and thrown at the receptionist? Well, that's the pig Flo stared at. Poor thing was still there. Flo continued to stare for a long time at the pig. Floyd was right. Even though it made her angry to admit it. Flo was convinced that I had been put to sleep. She had seen the big sign in the entry hall about the three and five day rule. Flo hated everybody who worked in the place.

"These horrible people have destroyed my $500.00." She mumbled to herself. Flo marched out and sat in her car for about twenty minutes, plotting revenge. Then suddenly, with a jerk of her head, she bolted from the car and headed back to the shelter.

What was she up to?

Chapter 7.

A WILD ROMP

Flo's plan was a fake, a flimflam, a hair-brained, bad idea. This time Floyd was not around to protect her from herself.

Flo walked right up to the reception desk and put on a honey of an act.

"My name if Flo Fevers. Someone stole my Pot Bellied pig right out of my front yard yesterday. Do you think it might be here?"

"We have one here. What did yours look like?" the receptionist asked.

Flo then gave the description of the pig back in the pen. The one she had just looked at. The pig's identification card stated that it had been surrendered to the Humane Society yesterday, Flo remembered.

"It happened yesterday," she lied.

It only took a few minutes to pull it off. Flo even gave the shelter her true name, telephone

47

number and address. Pretty dumb. Don't you agree? This woman's head would make a small pile of rocks.

She shoved this pig in my plastic carrier in the trunk of her car before slamming down the lid and heading for home.

"Who cares if it isn't mine? No one will ever know the difference. It was free for the taking, and I took it. And now, Floyd, I'll get my money back. I'll sell this one."

"Flo, you worry me! What you have done is wrong. What if the owner comes looking for that pig? What if you've make him mad? He might come here and slap you around and shoot up the place. Who knows!" Floyd was nervous.

"What if, what if! Shut up, Floyd. You are upsetting me," Flo shouted. "This is my pig now. It is my answer to a problem, a way to recoup my investment. I *will* get my money back, one way or the other.

This is my favorite part of the telling of this story. We can add to the list one more thing that Flo did not understand. This pig was not like me. This was a wild pig. Flo, not knowing any better, carried the cage into the hallway, set it down and opened the door.

No horse ever came out of the starting gate with more gusto! The pig raced through the house like a Kansas cyclone. He leaped over the coffee table. Expensive musical carousels flew in a million directions, crashing loudly on the floor. A small rocker lay dead-looking, on its side.

His first trip through the living room was only the beginning. He was just getting warmed up. Over went the brass lamp. The weight of it struck the thirty gallon aquarium hard enough to break the glass. Lovely blue and yellow fish fell to the rug and flopped helplessly. On the second trip through, he ate the yellow fish and rooted the blue one over Flo's foot.

Both Flo and Floyd hotfooted behind, trying to catch the pig. But the pig was smart and swift. It jumped up on the couch, rooted off all the pillows and tried to climb the wall. Down went a gold, metal framed mirror, crashing behind the couch. The noise frightened the pig. He ran around back of the entertainment center. Somehow he got tangled up in all the electrical cords back there. Over went the video tape cabinet.

Flo tried to trap him on one end of the cabinet and Floyd on the other. The pig squealed at the top of his lungs. Now he was scared. So scared he chose that spot to go to the bathroom. It was awful. Floyd got hold of the pig's hind leg. It was not clean. Floyd hung on anyway. He lifted the pig out, but the pig's leg was so slick with manure. Floyd could not hold on. Pig sprang forth with renewed energy.

Luckily for them, a most unusual thing happened. Old Gus sauntered in from the porch. The noise had become sufficiently loud to wake him, even though he is old and very hard of hearing. But this racket was sufficiently loud to disturb even the dead.

The pig saw Gus. Never having seen a bull dog before, he stared and gaped at Gus. And stared. And stared. All this was a big mistake for the pig.

Flo picked him up and threw him back in my cage. Then she sat down on the floor, kicked her feet like a spoiled child, and screamed.

Floyd went to work, cleaning up.

The pig spent the night in the garage. Floyd picked up everything he thought the pig might destroy before turning him loose from the carrier.

After Floyd and Flo had gone to bed upstairs, Floyd's nephew, Brian, arrived, just as he does two nights a week. Brian goes to work with Floyd on a construction job.

No one had warned Brian about the pig. When he opened the garage door the pig ran out. It was dark so Brian did not notice. Being tired, he went straight up to bed.

Pig found some wonderful places to root and play, all around the house. A bulldozer could have done no better. The greatest fun was the newly planted iris bed. The earth was fresh and soft from all the steer manure. Roots flew in every direction as the pig buried his nose deep in the soil. Pig was in no hurry. It was a warm spring evening. The moon had not yet come up over the hills behind the house, so it was fairly dark out there.

Accidentally, the pig slipped into the fish pond. As it turned out, he liked it a lot. The little fountain in the center spit out clean, fresh water. Pig turned his head up to catch a mouthful. Splashing around in the water cooled his belly and wet him good, all over. Well soaked, we went back to play in the soft steer manure of the iris bed. The manure began to stick, in layers, to his happy, wet, little body.

When he grew tired of it all , he began searching for an open door to get back into the house. Floyd had built a pet opening by the back kichen door for Gus. Gus was coming out. Clever Pig watched. If a dog can come out, then a pig can go in. So, out came Gus, In went Pig, mud, steer manure and all.

Everyone was sound asleep upstairs. You would think the pig would stumble around in the dark for a couple of minutes, find a spot and go to sleep. Fat chance! Some other pig might, but not this fun loving rascal. This pig thrived on mischief.

A little night light was on in the kitchen. Sufficient for the pig. First, he sniffed out the floor for any fallen scraps. Finding none, he scouted around. The brass knobs on the cupboard doors were quite handy. The pig was sure they were there for his convenience. With one twitch of his nose, the door flew open wide.

Aha! Food! Right in front of his eyes sat half a

a blue box of C & H powdered sugar. Nobody was looking. One nudge and the box was on the floor and so was the sugar. How sweet, how fun! He lapped some up and smeared some around. Behind that box was another. This one was brown in color, C & H brown sugar, unopened. No problem for a skillful pig like this creature. Pig found he didn't care too much for the brown sugar, so he just rooted it a-round, sort of mixing it up with the white sugar. The brown stuck to the bottoms of his feet.

Pig literally raided and trashed all the lower cup-boards. Food in hard plastic and glass containers was safe. Paper boxes and plastic bags offered little chal-lenge. He tried Wheaties and Grape Nut Flakes, rai-sins, dried prunes and apricots, almonds, chocolate chips, oh, were they great, and fig newtons. The long spaghetti broke open and rolled across the kitchen floor like pickup sticks. The jumbo macaroni was fun. It crunched and popped under his feet and got stuck between his toes.

An hour later, this shameless, full-bellied rogue trotted into the living room, climbed upon the yellow velvet couch and dropped off to sleep.

Not only was he mud and manure caked, add to that white and brown sugar. A little of everything he had eaten was stuck to the mud. He looked like he had rolled in garbage before he stretched himself out on the couch. His wet hair had turned everything into a stinking paste. Before the sun came up he had slept all over the couch. The white lace pillows had turned into a barf colored goo.

Flo came down the stairs to start breakfast. Bedlam was about to break loose. Every breath of air in the house was tense with expectation.

A fowl odor tainted the morning air. Flo's head was tilted back, sniffing. Then, she stepped into the kitchen. Her stockinged feet began to slip in the goo. As quick as a lightning flash, her bottom hit the floor. She screamed, wildly. Both hands hit the floor in an effort to get out of the mess. As quick as they went down, both hands came back up, full of the putrid mixture. Flo screamed again for Floyd.

Floyd and his nephew ran down the stairs to see what was wrong.

"Flo?" Floyd yelled. "Where are you?"

"Where do you think I am? I'm in the kitchen, you big dummy!" she screeched.

The sleeping beauty on the couch was disturbed by the racket, but not enough to get up yet.

Brian looked at his Aunt Flo sitting there on the floor in the slop. Now she splashed with both hands, in anger. Brian began to laugh, uncontrollably. The harder he tried to stop, the funnier Flo looked to him.

Floyd spotted the pig lying on the couch and staring toward the kitchen. Now, Floyd began to laugh.

Flo's hands were full of the putrid mixture.
She screamed for Floyd.

It was knee slapping, cackling time.

Both Brian and Floyd were near convulsions.

Flo was getting angrier by the minute. Finally, when she could stand it no more she commenced to scream at the top of her lungs!

"Stop it! Stop it! It's not funny! Get me out of here!"

That did it. Pig took a flying leap off the couch and headed for the kitchen. Seeing Flo sitting there startled him for a second, but only a second. The pig slipped right on in and began to slurp up the slop. He had left some of the dried fruit and fig newtons; he probably left them for breakfast.

When Floyd caught his breath, he said to his wife what any self respecting husband would say at a time like this.

"Flo, you got yourself into this mess ---"

Brian interupted, still convulsed with laughter. "And you can sure see she's in a mess all right!"

"And Flo," Floyd continued, "you can get yourself out of it."

With that bit of advice, Floyd and Brian got dressed and left for work. Floyd, on second thought, stuck his head back in the door. "Oh, Flo, don't bother to make breakfast. Brian and I will eat at the Truck Stop."

Flo grabbed a handful of garbage and threw it at the door. She must have sat there in the mess for another half hour feeling sorry for herself. The pig had the free run of the house.

How could she ever get $500.00 out of this house-wrecking pig? Flo would not give up. What would she try next?

Chapter 8.

LUCY ENJOYS THE FARM

I hope you learned from Flo's terrible experience. Unless you know what kind of a pig you are dealing with, don't bring one in your house and turn it loose. All pigs don't behave as well as I do. Flo found that out and got what she deserved for taking that pig from the Humane Society in the first place.

Later, we learned that the pig's name was "Wrecker". Now you have an idea why his owner brought him to the Humane Society and threw him at the receptionist. Makes me wonder how much damage he did at home.

As for me, I was having the time of my life, except for the nightmares. Once in a while Mama heard me thrashing around in my sleep and came to quiet me down. She would wake me up and tell me it was only a bad dream. Once, while I was napping, I

dreamed I was still at the Humane Society. It was the
third day and I couldn't find my harness. I looked
everywhere for it, but I could not find it anywhere,
My gate flew open. There stood a skeleton faced man
in a long blue coat. In his hand was a big ax held high
over his head. I knew he was going to kill me. I must
have yelled out in my sleep. Mama came and petted
me. She said, "It's only a dream, Lucy. Don't worry.
You are safe here with us. Go back to sleep and
dream about good things to eat. Think about what it
will be like when the apple trees are loaded with fresh
red fruit." I tried it. It worked. Mama certainly
knows her pigs.

Papa and Mama knew everything there was to
know about raising farm hogs. I had met all of theirs.
What a healthy, happy bunch. The four-week-old pigs
are bigger than full grown Pot Bellies. I had to laugh
when I saw them. They couldn't believe I was over
three months old.

I heard Papa tell Mama that these pigs were push-
ing about 40 pounds. Strange. No wonder they call
us mini-pigs. My mother was three years old when I
was born. She weighed 53 pounds and was 15" tall.

Of all the farm hogs, I liked Little Prissy best. She
is the kindest, most intelligent hog I have ever seen.
And, she liked me. I hoped we could be good friends.
"But maybe they will give me away before long. I
don't know what will happen to me. I'm not even

sure I want to know," I thought.

Papa spent a good deal of time trying to figure out what Pot Bellied pig breeders are doing wrong. He had lots to say at the supper table about what he would do differently.

"How can breeders sell their pigs as house pets if the pigs have never seen the inside of a house? That has to change. Their living quarters must at least resemble the home the pig will be moving in to. Before a pig leaves the breeder it must have spent time in the house. The way I see it, not only does the pig need training, but so does the owner. Sure would make for a happier arrangement."

"Too bad Papa didn't train Flo," I told Mama.

Mama was listening to what Papa had to say. She had some doubts. "If you are a big breeder with lots of little sows, it would be impossible to bring each pig in the house?"

"I thought about that. Folks like these little guys. I'll bet you could find a neighbor or two to hire when the load got heavy."

Mama agreed.

Supper smelled terrific. Flo never, ever handed me a crumb from the table. In this kitchen, it was pure heaven. Bites were always poked at me under the table, larger portions of greens and vegetables, tiny portions of sweets and starches. My diet was always tasty and healthful, a diet planned to keep me small and trim. No complaints.

"In the morning I think I will check with Pamela to see what has become of the new pig in the shelter," Mama said. "Could be it needs a home too."

Mama did not know that Flo had taken Wrecker home with her.

A brand new Pet Porter was placed in the corner of the den. It was just for me. There was plenty of room in it, with some air holes for good circulation and a nice metal see-through door. A door that didn't even get closed when we all went to bed. Papa cut a piece of thick carpeting to line the floor and Mama stuffed a warm blanket around me and said, "Good night, my little friend. If you need anything in the night, come into our bedroom and wake us up. It is O.K. with us."

I thanked her for her kindness to me. She reached in and gave me a hug. Me! A hug! I couldn't believe it. A hug, just for me.

The house was quiet. Much different than the Humane Society at night. Once I heard Maggie, the old Springer Spaniel barking at something. Papa got up to check the back yard.

Maggie slept in an enclosed porch in back of the kitchen. You could see her through the window. For a while there I thought that dog must have really long legs. She was always scratching on the window, making dirty streaks with her feet. Then one day I found out there was a dog house out there, under the window. It had a flat roof. That's what she was standing on to fool me. Her house was also carpeted and had an overhead heat lamp for cold nights, though I doubt it got very cold in that nice room.

"Can't have her old bones getting cold," I heard Papa say one night when the temperature dropped and he switched on the lamp.

Papa came by my bed after he checked to see what had caused Maggie to bark.

"Did she wake you up too, Lucy?" he asked. "Don't worry. It was only a few deer coming down out of the timber to drink from the water tank. Maggie thinks she has to tell us if anyone or anything gets too close."

I guess Papa was referring to the deer as "anything". It made me wonder if I was an "anything". Probably.

Other than hearing someone snore once, the rest of the night was very peaceful.

I got to slide down to the back yard while Mama was cooking breakfast. For a few minutes I rooted the fallen pine cones over by the fence. Maybe I would get to do that every day.

I had milk, some little grain pellets, a little bit of wheat toast and a handful of grapes. Afterwards Papa invited me to go along for a walk around the farm, but for some reason I was sleepy. I loved my bed.

About this time, something very funny was going on at the Humane Society. I wish I had been there to see it happen. Maybe Flo wasn't as clever as she thought.

Chapter 9.

WRECKER EXPLAINED

Betty McCall was ashamed of herself. She had been ashamed since the day she threw Wrecker at the receptionist then turned and walked out. She knew she must return to the Humane Society. Her purpose in coming back was to confess, and to take responsiblity for her actions. As naughty and destructive as Wrecker was, he was hers. She would take him back home and try to train him. She vowed to beg forgiveness of the good folks at the shelter, claim her pet and make an honest attempt to teach the little monster some manners. Betty had a kind heart; she had simply never been educated as to the responsiblilties of a pet pig owner.

Shyly she faced the receptionist.

"Do you remember me?" she asked. "Probably not! You were too busy catching the pig I practically threw at you."

The receptionist looked up and laughed. "Oh yes! I do remember you. In fact, I will never forget."

"I hope you will forgive me. I've come to take the naughty little scamp home. We call him 'Wrecker'." The name suits him perfectly. I have a list of things a mile long that this pig has destroyed. But my kids love the little rascal. My five year old, Tiffany, cried and sobbed for hours last night until I promised I'd bring him home. Actually, I'll hate myself for giving in. I just know I will."

"Can't you rig up a confinement area someplace until he's better trained?" the receptionist suggested, enjoying the funny predicament into which this lady had gotten herself.

"Most definitely!" she answered. "Wrecker will wear a permanent harness. When he is allowed out of confinement someone will hang on to him until he can be trusted to behave."

"You know something, we may have a problem here," the receptionist told her. She picked up the phone and asked for one of the animal handlers to come to the front desk.

Dave and Pamela both showed up about the same time.

"Tell me something. Am I mistaken or is the pig compartment empty?" she asked.

"No, that's correct. The one remaining pig was picked up yesterday by its owner," Dave answered.

"What?" Betty McCall exclaimed. "*I am the owner!*" What dummy would claim Wrecker?"

The receptionist sent for Mrs. Bates, the director. After a quick search the name of Flo Fevers emerged, along with the address, 825 Bodger Avenue and a telephone number.

Betty McMall began to laugh. Mrs. Bates felt somewhat relieved knowing the pig's owner, for some strange reason, was not upset. Indeed Betty found it funny.

"Let us in on the joke," Mrs. Bates said.

"You'd have to know Wrecker to understand my thinking. Whoever this Flo Fevers person is will soon have more than a 'fever'. Wrecker is a destroyer, bulldozer and Sherman tank, all rolled into one little pig! Don't be too concerned. She will bring him back, and soon. You can bet on it!" Betty told them convincingly. "Give it a few hours. That's all it will take. The pig will show up again and when he does, give me a call. I will come and get him."

"But Mrs. McCall, this woman came in here and took a pet that wasn't hers to take. What she did is illegal. Aren't you even angry about it? We have an officer here who can go out and give this woman a little trouble," Mrs. Bates explained.

Betty began to laugh again. "Believe me when I tell you, Mrs. Bates, she is already in trouble. Wrecker by this time will have dealt severely with her. No judge could hand out punishment more fitting than she is going through right now."

Boy! Did Betty McCall know her pig, or what? She was confident as she left the shelter with a gigantic grin on her face. Wrecker's return was inevitable; on that she would bet her mother's dentures.

Meanwhile, the activity at Flo's house continued. I can't wait to tell you about it.

Flo coaxed Wrecker to the garage with Hershey's chocolate syrup. One more flavor to add to his filthy, smelly, garbage-caked body.

If the bath room had been able to do so, it would have groaned when it saw Flo coming. Some of everything on the pig was also on Flo. The tub had never seen or smelled so much filth on one human being.

Flo soaked. The smart thing to do would have been to stand up and shower away the gunk. That was the sensible thing to do, but as usual, common sense was not Flo's long suit. Now the garbage was floating on top of the water, sailing all around the tub. The odor was disgusting. The particles stuck to the sides of the tub and stuck under Flo's arm pits as well.

As if to tantalize Flo, a little brown spider let itself down from the ceiling on a strong, thin line, halting and swaying from side to side, about three inches from her nose.

The spider was the last straw. Flo was terrified of

spiders. The bug was not affected by Flo's shrieks, but by the air coming from her mouth. Fortunately, Flo did not suck the spider down her throat when she drew in oxygen. The bug drew up about a foot and hesitated. Flo leaned back. She looked up at the spider. The little bug bounced, throwing Flo into fits of squealing. She put her hands together to ask God to protect her from this frightful pest.

Slowly, the spider crawled up its lead line and let the nervous woman in the bathtub return to the problem that surrounded her in the water.

Several times the water had to be changed and the garbage scraped from the bottom of the tub. All this took the better part of two hours. When the job was done, Flo concluded that she was the only clean thing in the house.

Using the yellow pages, Flo found a listing that raised her spirits somewhat. "The Lilly White Cleaners, we clean anything and everything". Flo certainly needed "everything" cleaned. She got the company to promise to send a couple of people over right away.

She figured she'd get them to bathe the pig after they had finished with the house. Do you suppose anyone is hard up enough for money to bathe that pig? What is to become of Wrecker?

Chapter 10.

PREPARING FOR PIGS

Papa and Arley Willett were playing at carpenter work and enjoying themselves immensely. Their plans had first been drawn on a large piece of white cardboard and tacked to the wall across the hall. A few of the unused hog pens were being converted into individual apartment for pigs like me. I must be expecting a lot of company.

Mama looked over Papa's plans. "Golly, these plans look like play houses for children, the kind I always dreamed of having when I was a little girl. And here you are, Papa, building my dream house for some Pot Bellied pigs." She laughed about it. So did Papa and Arley.

The farrowing barn was a long structure, built to last. Two rows of ten foot square pens were separated by a wide hallway. Nowadays only a few of the front pens were in use. There were many empty pens to choose from for the remodeling. To begin the project, Papa had selected a couple of pens located about thirty feet from the farm hogs. If they were too far away from the front door it would take more time to get to them. The back door was another two hundred feet away. I told you it was a big, long building.

The newly remodeled pens were never to be called pens, but rather apartments. Each apartment would consist of two 10' by 5' rooms. The carpeted front room would resemble as nearly as possible a living room-bedroom combination. The back room would not be quite so fancy. This floor would be wood plank, where food and water could be served. A small back door opened to the out-of-doors, a private covered area, dry in the winter with plenty of spots for sun bathing. Best of all, the enclosure provided an outdoor place to go to the bathroom.

Papa said he needed Mama's know-how with the decorating. "These small apartments must not look anything like pig pens. When the pig moves into a house, it must feel at home. So, how about some nice indoor paint and wallpaper?"

"Wallpaper? Papa, are you sure about that?" Mama laughed, ..."You always tease me about carrying on conversations with the pigs and now here you are, wanting to hang wallpaper for them. Anyone would think we're nuts."

Papa just smiled and kept on with his planning.

"You and I are going to Salem to the Eastside Auction to look for some good used furniture. The small kind. We will buy small television sets, radios, lamps, carpet, little tables and pillows, anything we can find to gussy up these pig apartments. We want them to feel right at home. O.K.?"

On the way to the house, Mama mulled over all the things Papa had told her. Maybe he was overdoing it. So what? He was enjoying fixing up for the pigs. "No animal ever had a better friend that my husband," she told herself.

I met Mama at the kitchen door. She asked me if I had had a nice nap.

"Yes, thank you," I answered. Anything was better than trying to sleep at the Humane Society, with all that barking going on.

"You'll be alone sometimes, honey." she told me. "I hope you won't mind. Papa and I have some shopping to do and some auctions to attend. The new apartments in the farrowing barn need things. I hope I don't forget and call them 'hog pens'. An old habit is hard to break."

"Do you think Little Prissy and her friend will be offended when they see the special treatment being given to us Pot Bellies?" I asked.

Mama stared at me. For a moment I thought I had asked a bad question.

"Oh my, Lucy, you are one thoughtful pig," she

said to me. "No, so far I hadn't given that much thought. How kind you are. Sometimes you remind me of Priscilla. You've heard us talk about her. She was a kind pig too, Lucy."

"Do you miss her?" I asked.

"Every day of my life I think about her," Mama said sadly.

That afternoon Papa and Mama went to Salem. They left the color television on for me and several layers of newspapers were spread on the floor in the kitchen, just in case. I hoped I could wait until they came home and let me out. How I wanted to please Mama and Papa!

The shopping turned out to be a lot of fun. Mama found some pretty yellow flowered wallpaper and paint to match. She bought yellow material for curtains.

After a couple of hours of serious shopping they drove over to Deana's house, their daughter who lives in Salem. Steven, Deana's youngest, is nine now.

"He'll want to go to the farm this week end when he finds out you have a new pig," Deana told them.

"That's great!" Papa replied. "But Steven will have to understand that Lucy is not ours. She is temporary until we can find a proper home for her. Steven gets attached to all the animals pretty quickly."

Deana's kids were all in school. Fourteen year old Shawn was busy with sports and scouting. Sara was sixteen and wanted to be an auto mechanic. Papa says she's too pretty to work in a garage. She also loves racing and race cars. Christina was away at college.

The next thing Papa and Mama did was to go to the Olive Garden, an Italian restaurant, to have some dinner before the auction which began at 6:30 p.m. I love pasta. They didn't bring me one bite.

Eastside Auction is a great place to buy almost anything. No two auctions are ever the same. The friendly family who runs the auction barn strive to make it a fun place.

By nine o'clock Papa had purchased a large roll of new tan carpeting for $15.00 and a small television for $17.50. A five dollar bill bought a radio, two metal buckets and a box of bath towels. Luckily, from an estate being auctioned, they were able to pick up several nice, large pet porters for little money. It was the first time they had ever seen pet carriers at the auction, so they bought them all.

"Can't tell when they'll come in handy," Papa said. "God only knows how may pigs we will end up with, so we had better be prepared."

As they were about to leave, two chairs and a ceiling fan were put up for sale. The chairs matched the wallpaper. So another $25.00 bit the dust.

By the time the boys at the auction got everything loaded on the pickup, the truck bed was piled high.

"What have we gotten ourselves into?" Mama asked as they pulled away from the auction. "Will everybody bring their unwanted pigs to us, Papa? What will happen then?"

Chapter 11.

APARTMENTS

Lori Beasley was on the phone talking to Papa for quite a while. She had purchased two Pot Bellied pigs from an unscrupulous man. One of the pigs was sick when she bought it. The poor thing died the next day. When she went back to demand another pig, the fellow became very angry, but he did end up giving her a replacement. Lori had been told to full feed the pigs. That means give them all they want to eat. She asked Papa if that was good advice. Papa told her it was good advice only if she wanted another dead pig on her hands. He also told her to go see Dr. Mike.

"Why are people calling me about Pot Bellied pigs? A few days ago, I didn't know much about them myself. I hope that woman doesn't kill her pigs. She is one more case of a person getting a pig before knowing a darn thing about how to take care of one.

I blame the breeder. Makes me mad," Papa fumed.

Papa was eager to get back to work on the apartments. The first one had been completed in two days. Once inside it, you would never know you were smack dab in the middle of a hog barn. It was very nice.

One of the new pet porters from the auction sat on the spot designated for sleeping. In this fancy place, there would be no hay for bedding. The tan carpet in the pet porter matched the carpet in the front room of the apartment. Even the blanket in the pet porter matched the rug.

I curled up on a large pillow in the corner of the apartment and watched the little television while Mama and Papa admired their creation. Arley had built a heavy table for the television so the pigs couldn't push it over. He had painted it yellow to match the curtains and trim.

"Have we forgotten anything?" Mama asked.

"Yes. Mats!" Papa answered. "Door mats. I want one at the front, inside the door and one in the back so they can wipe their feet when they come in from the outside."

"I didn't know pigs were smart enough to wipe their feet on a mat until I saw Priscilla do it," Mama laughed.

I didn't like the remark about pigs not being smart enough. I gave Mama a dirty look.

"Sorry Lucy. I just meant that pigs aren't usually expected to wipe their feet. But if you are going to be living in the house, your owner will be a lot happier if you wipe your feet before going in. On the other hand, if we don't show the pigs what the mats are to be used for, they will just root them around. And that's a fact."

A heavy marble dish was in the back room for water and a nine-inch cake pan was setting there as a temporary feed pan. It bothered me having something in common with a feed pan, I am temporary, too.

"We still have a lot to learn about these pigs," Papa said. "At any rate, we will be ready to help Pamela the next time one comes in, homeless or abused. There is no reason why a pig has to be put to sleep when we have the time and space to help out. Here is what I plan to do. When we pick up a pig we'll take it by the vet for a check up to make sure it's healthy. Arley is preparing and isolation pen for sick pigs. As soon as we can we will take it into the house, or put it in an apartment and train it, if it needs training. The kids can help with that. Steven will love it. Then we will put the word out that we have pigs who need good homes. But there's one catch, who ever gets a pig from us won't be allowed to take it off the place until 'they', the owners, have been trained. Several times they must come and handle the pig and learn everything we can teach them about care and feeding.

And before they can handle the pig, we will set them down in a classroom, over there," he pointed to a large pen. "We will fix it up with a video tape to do the training for us."

"Where are you going to get such a tape?" Mama asked.

"I've seen them advertised. If we can't find one we like, we'll just make our own."

Arley came by the apartment. "Well, this is cozy. If this is a house warming, where is the cake?" he smiled.

"Come on in, Arley, and pull up a pillow," Papa invited.

"I thought I'd begin on the next little house now that the chores are done. Well, hello pig!" Arley spoke to me, seeing me there on the pillow. "Are you happy to be out of the Humane Society?"

"Yes, I am!" I answered.

"She sure is." Mama told him. Arley knew about Mama. He hears her talking to hogs all the time. Arley said it was a special gift. Mama told him as far as she was concerned, I could stay out here or I could stay in the house. "This sweet little thing can do as she likes," she said. That was nice.

I kept telling myself not to get my hopes up. A great place like this could never be my permanent home. It was too much to hope for. But sometimes, for a little while, I would dream about it. I knew why

Mama and Papa were going to all this trouble. They love pigs and want to help out. As soon as someone wanted me and had been properly trained, I'd be out of here.

"If I had just one wish, you know what it would be, but I will never be that lucky," I thought sadly.

Papa and Arley walked down to Patsy's pen to see her new litter of fourteen pigs, born during the night. Remember, Patsy is a farm hog.

I was glad they left. Now, I could talk to Mama. "How many little apartments will Papa build?" I asked.

"I'm not too sure, Lucy. About three or four, I guess. We have enough carpet for that many and paint too, I think. Next auction night Papa and I will try to pick up some more furnishings and televisions."

"Sometimes I'd like to stay out here, but I sure do like it in the house," I told Mama. She said the choice was up to me. I hoped she would say she liked having me in the house, but she didn't.

We walked past the big hogs before leaving the barn. They were a happy lot. I knew they thought I was a funny looking pig; I really didn't care because I thought the same about them.

Little Prissy was super. She always spoke kindly to me. Mama greeted each of the farm hogs and asked a sow named Penny about her babies. Four days ago

Penny and her new litter.

she had had a litter of fourteen. Two of her babies were quite small and were being fed bottles of goat milk. Mama said the goat milk was doing a good job. Patsy and her fourteen babies were sound asleep.

"What's going on down there?" Prissy asked. "What's all that hammering about?"

Mama took a few minutes to explain to the intelligent sow about the Pot Bellied pig apartments.

"My goodness," Prissy replied. "I think you started something when you took my mother in the house. Now everybody wants a pet pig."

Mama laughed. "But everybody shouldn't have one, Prissy, unless they know something about pigs. Too many of them are neglected and end up in the Humane Society, like Lucy did."

I asked Little Prissy if I could come and visit her sometimes. She smiled and said I could come anytime I wanted to, that she loved company.

A couple of big hogs across the hall were listening. They didn't want me here; I could tell by the dirty looks they gave me. I became aware of their size. Will they cause trouble for the Pot Bellies in the barn? At night, Mama and Papa won't be around to protect us.

Chapter 12.

CLEANING UP THE MESS

Two cleaning companies came to Flo's house and refused to clean up the mess. The first cleaning women left, holding their noses. One of them handed out dusting cloths to cover their faces. The other made disgusting gagging noises, even as the car hurried away. An hour later, a man and his wife arrived and carted in cleaning supplies. Five minutes later they were nowhere in sight. The wife yelled back over her shoulder at Flo.

"Call the fire department, have them hose out the house; no, better than that, just set a match to the house."

Finally, a young couple, John and Jean Turner, just getting started in the business and needing the money badly, stayed and did the job. They wore face masks while they worked. The masks were not quite adequate in keeping out the stink. Regardless of how badly they needed the work, even these folks drew the line when it came to bathing Wrecker.

Flo had turned up the heat in the house so high it was 100 degrees in there. She was trying to dry the carpet where the aquarium had broken and spilled. Besides that, she brought in two small floor heaters and a large electric fan, all pointed toward the wet spot.

All that electricity being used at the same time was too much for the power system. A circuit breaker kicked off and everything shut down, expect Flo. Flo panicked.

The cleaning people, half sick from working in all that smell and heat, were packing up their old van as quickly as they could, trying to get away. They were tired and sweaty and had earned every penny of their money. Flo had not bothered to give them a cent extra over their hourly scale. After a job like this, they both asked themselves how soon they could get out of this business and into another.

Flo ran out to them and begged for help with the electricity. It was no big deal, really. In a matter of minutes, John Turner had the power back on, after unplugging a heater.

"Don't plug it back in, Lady, unless you want the same thing to happen again," John told her. "You've got enough heat in there already to dry up the Mississippi River."

Flo begged them to wash the pig. Jean almost gave in because of the money. John took a deep breath. "I'll help you put the pig in the tub but you have to wash it!"

Flo refused his offer. She vowed she would not touch that pig, ever.

When the van pulled away, the day was spent. Floyd phoned to say that he and Brian would eat in town. Neither of them was eager to listen to Flo.

Gail Snoopy hurried across the street to see her neighbor. She peeked through the garage window looking for Flo. What she saw was something that resembled a pig, except this thing looked like it had been dropped in the garbage bucket and baked. Flo was standing there holding her apron over her nose and mouth staring at the thing.

Gail tapped on the window. Flo came to the front door.

"What happened to Lucy?" Gail asked.

"That pig is not Lucy!" Flo snapped.

"Not Lucy? Don't tell me you bought another pig. How did it get so filthy?" the neighbor asked.

"The Humane Society destroyed Lucy! I made them give me another pig," Flo lied. She would have been furious if she had known I was alive and having a great time out on the farm.

"This pig," Flo bellowed, "practically wrecked my home. I'm calling my lawyer. Nobody does this to me and gets away with it, nobody! I plan to sue the Humane Society!"

Gail knew how Flo stretched the truth. She did not know what to believe. Yet, Gail wondered if the Humane Society really had destroyed me. I always liked Gail and her twins. They liked me too. The twins sometimes shared their little boxes of raisins with me.

Wrecker did not get any dinner. Flo shouted at the pig, saying "You'll never get another bite of food from this house." Actually, he had already eaten almost everything she had in the house. She wouldn't feed the pig and she wouldn't bathe it. After all, he didn't deserve a bath and after all, I kinda doubt if Wrecker was hungry. What Flo really wanted to do was get rid of the pig. She didn't care how! Maybe Floyd might have an idea as to what to do with Wrecker.

On the contrary, when Floyd and Brian returned home, Floyd made it perfectly clear to his wife that he wanted nothing to do with her pig problems.

"I'll get a lawyer," she told Floyd.

"Get a lawyer? Flo, you stole that pig! It isn't yours! You deserve everything that pig can dish out. Now I don't want to hear any more about it."

Brian listened. He felt sorry for the poor, filthy little porker running around in the garage. When Flo and Floyd were interested in the television that night, he slipped into the kitchen, got a pan of water and some leftovers and snuck out to the garage, being careful to close the door behind him. Wrecker was happy to get the food and water. A pig always loves to eat.

The pig smelled worse than the fish market. One eye was completely caked over with mud. Gobs of each of the foods he had gotten into were dried and stuck to the filth on his body. The funniest looking was the long string of dried spaghetti stuck to his tail. Each time he switched his tail the spaghetti made a tapping sound on the floor.

"Listen, Stinky," Brian said to the pig. "I wish I could stay and visit, but you really are hard on my nose." Wrecker probably understood.

The next morning a great thing happened. Mrs. Bates called. Flo realized her plot had failed.

"Mrs. Fevers, you picked up a Pot Bellied pig from us, claiming it was yours."

Flo was caught. Like a caged animal she struck back. "That pig tore up my place. I've a good mind to sue you."

"Mrs. Fevers, if you don't return that pig to us immediately, you are going to get more than sued. The sheriff will be knocking on your door."

Now, Flo was scared. She hung up and began plotting again. "I'll take the filthy pig back to them. It will serve them right. Anyway, it's time I go down there and give them a piece of my mind for destroying my $500.00."

Quickly she put on a pair of Floyd's gloves and loaded Wrecker in my pet porter, which she placed in the trunk of her car and drove to the Humane Society.

Immediately, Alanna Scanlon, the receptionist at the Humane Society, recognized her. She rang for Mrs. Bates.

Flo was so flustered, she wasn't sure what to do. Nevertheless, she put on quite an act.

"I'm so sorry about the mix up. I have come to return the pig I thought was mine. This one is a real terror." As Flo rattled on, hoping to overwhelm the receptionist, she did not notice that Mrs. Bates had entered the room.

Mrs. Bates listened carefully as she stood behind Flo. Then she came around and faced Flo squarely.

"Mrs. Fevers," she began, "I am Mrs. Bates, the administrator of the Humane Society. I don't think you ever owned a pig. I think you just came in here and claimed someone else's pet. Isn't that true?"

"How dare you accuse me? You don't know what you are talking about," Flo spouted back. "I do have a lost pig. I've been so upset about it, I thought this one was mine, but it isn't. The pig is in the trunk of my car. If you want it, come out and get it." Flo turned and stomped out.

The foul aroma from the pig soiled the noonday air.

Lonnie Long and Doris Sipes followed her out to the car. When Flo opened the trunk, the foul aroma from the pig soiled the noonday air.

"There he is! Take him before I get sick!" Flo coughed and covered her mouth.

Pamela came out to check on the situation. "How did this pig get so filthy? He looks like he fell in a garbage dump."

"How did you guess?" Flo snapped, "*And I am going to sue this place!*"

"*Oh yeah!*" Pam replied. "When Mrs. Bates gets through with you, I don't think you'll be suing anybody!"

Flo put her hands on her hips and glared at Pam.

"Will this pig end up with your friends over in Thomas Creek, too?" Doris asked Pam, innocently.

That was the wrong thing to ask in front of Flo, who was listening.

"No, this rascal has an owner." Pam answered, holding her nose.

Lonnie slipped a leash around Wrecker's neck and lead him into the Humane Society.

"So, the pigs in here go to her friends in Thomas Creek, huh? Well, isn't that interesting." Flo wondered if maybe I was at Thomas Creek, too. Maybe I was still alive, she told herself.

The woman was determined to find out. She did not care a thing about me, but she was determined to get her money back. Was it possible that this strange person could gather up enough smarts to find me? We shall see.

Chapter 13

SWEET JASMINE

At the farm, the next few days were full of fun and excitement. The grandsons, Shawn and Steven, came to visit. I got to run around with them all over the place. We went swimming in Mill Creek. I didn't even know I could swim. Later, Shawn caught four trout in about 20 minutes. Back in the timber, Steven was busy chasing squirrels up trees and thumping rabbits out of hollow logs. I got to root around a lot. I was the one who discovered all the mushrooms, lots of them. Shawn took off his T-shirt and tied a knot in the bottom of it. It made a great bag for hauling the mushrooms to Mama's kitchen. Shawn said he learned that in Boy Scouts. I had heard mushrooms are better cooked. Maybe I would find out!

Papa and Arley built six apartments before they decided to stop. Mama said each one was cuter than the other. I don't know what that means.

Papa and Mama had been back to Eastside Auction to buy more furniture and televisions and stuff. When Papa told the auctioneer he was furnishing apartments for Pot Bellied pigs, the auctioneer thought he was joking. But one morning when Papa had to make another trip back to the auction to pick up the rest of his load, I got to ride along.

Papa said to the auctioneer, "Dick, this is one of the pigs we built an apartment for."

"You're serious?" he laughed.

Papa realized how funny it sounded. But he didn't care.

When we got home, Mama had news from the Humane Society.

"Someone reported a family who was starving their pig. The family claimed they threw feed down but their dog gobbled it up pretty fast. I guess they weren't too upset when investigative officer picked up the pig. It's at the shelter. I told them we would come in and get it Monday morning, O.K.?" she asked.

"Sure, we'll go get it," Papa grinned.

Steven jumped up and down! "Another pig, another pig!"

"Gosh Steven," his brother said, "What's so unusual about one more pig on this place? Almost every time we visit there are new pigs."

"I know, but these Pot Bellies are different. They are small, like toys, and Lucy will have a friend. Friends are very important," Steven said seriously.

Actually, I tried not to get too excited about anything. I've learned it's better not to get excited about good news. Who knows? At any moment things can change. Tomorrow I might be out of here and it would be just my luck. I tried not to think about it.

Mrs. Bates and Pamela were on hand at the Humane Society to greet Mama and Papa.

"How are you getting along with Little Miss Pot Belly?" Pam asked.

"Great!" Mama told them. "We thought about bringing her with us, but I think she might not want to see this place for a while."

"You are probably right," Mrs. Bates agreed. "This place can be pretty awful for an animal sometimes. We do the best we can," she said sadly. "This new pig we picked up needs vittles. I believe she is healthy enough."

"Don't worry. We will fix her up in no time," Papa replied.

Once in the office, Papa let Mrs. Bates and Pamela in on all the plans and progress on the farm.

"We had no idea you'd do all that," Pamela told Papa. "I should have known."

"There are six apartments, so far. We hope that will be enough. Arley is building a special room now for the orientation of pet pig owners. By the time we get through with them, they will know a little bit more about taking care of a pig, and if they really do want one for a pet, or not."

The little girl pig was skin and bones, but she was house broken. That was a plus. But this one was trained to a darned old kitty litter box, like I was. Well, I guess that's better than the floor.

"What did the owners call her?" Mama asked.

"They called her Slops," Pamela said. "Isn't that awful?"

"Oh, it's horrid! Shameful! Well, she will never be 'Slops' again," Mama said to the hungry looking pig in her arms. There is no justice in a name like that. We will make it up to her. Her name should be something like Justice, or Jussy, perhaps Jasmine. I'll have to see what fits her best."

I heard the car pull in when they returned home. Maybe now someone would answer the phone. For the past hour it had rung continually.

Papa's arms were full of groceries. Mama's load was not so big. She held a skinny little pig that weighed about half of what it should. Before she put it on the floor she snapped a blue leash around its neck and took it up under the big pine tree.

"You don't have to use a litter box anymore, honey. Those things are for cats, or emergencies. You can come out here anytime you have to," Mama told her.

Two bowls of milk sat waiting on the kitchen floor, one for me and one for the new pig. When I saw how hungry she was and how fast she devoured her milk, I told her she could have mine too. She polished them off, quickly. I felt sorry for her as she stood by the bowl in hopes more food was coming. Papa made her happy by throwing a couple of big handfuls of pellets in the dish. She quickly scarfed them down and waited a few minutes more. Seeing nothing else was offered to eat, she began to snoop.

My bed in the pet porter was the only pig bed in the house, so far. Where would she sleep?

Papa had a suggestion. "Lucy, let's take her ---"

Mama interupted. "Sweet Jasmine. Let's call her Sweet Jasmine. After a name like 'Slops' she deserves a sweet name."

Papa picked up the pig. With a full belly, she felt a bit heavier. "How about it, pig, is Sweet Jasmine to your liking?"

The pig did not utter a sound. She wasn't very sociable.

"Lucy, as I was about to say, let's take Sweet Jasmine down to the farrowing barn and introduce her to a new apartment."

"Are you sure this little thing ought to be alone?" Mama was concerned.

"We will all keep a close eye on her. If it doesn't

work out, we can always bring her back in the house for a while."

"I just figured she would be in the house a little longer," Mama sounded disappointed.

"Mama you worry too much," Papa told her as we left the house. I was grateful for Papa's invitation. I had to hurry to keep up with him as we walked through the apple orchard to the barn. I don't know if Sweet Jasmine enjoyed being carried to the barn or not. Nary a word came out of her. How strange!

The farm hogs heard us coming. Several of them hurried to their feet to get a better look at us. We passed by their pens going to the apartments.

Once again I felt about as small as a flea, around the farm hogs. It's kinda scary. Once Papa pointed out some three month old feeder pigs in the big building. He said they averaged about ninety pounds, he thought. That's a lot. Mama held me on her bathroom scales and then announced to me that I weighed eleven and a half pounds. If one of these hogs ever gets mad at me and gets out, I'm making tracks.

While Papa flipped channels on the television in the apartment, looking for cartoons or music, which is what pigs like, I showed Sweet Jasmine around her new place. First I took her to the outside pen. She raced around in it and chose a bathroom corner, just like she was supposed to. Papa poured fresh water in a new metal pan.

I thought I had better reassure Sweet Jasmine. "No dog will eat your food or drink your water here," I told her. "Papa would never allow that to happen."

She gave no reply. In fact, she didn't even look at me.

When Papa opened the little door for me to leave with him, I ran the other way.

"O.K., stay with her for a while, Lucy," he said.

I figured if I could get this pig to trust me, she might talk. I tried my best. I spoke kindly to her and asked simple questions, but Sweet Jasmine did not answer. Maybe she was snooty. The way she acted, she didn't hear a word I said. Maybe she couldn't! Was that possible? Only one time I heard a strange, quiet grunt out of her. But it didn't sound like any hog sound I had ever heard before.

After she lay down in her pet porter, I rattled the metal door. She didn't grunt once. A pig always grunts! At least once.

I would have to ask Mama. Was it possible for someone not to speak or hear? How awful. Maybe no one will ever want her. What will become of us?

Chapter 14.

BABY PIGS ON THE KITCHEN FLOOR

Have you ever had that feeling that something bad was about to happen? You look around to see if someone is staring at your back and no one is there? Well, I had had that feeling for several days. It was so real, I dreaded getting up in the morning.

The first night she was there, I slept in an apartment next door to Sweet Jasmine. I watched her. I don't think she ever got lonesome. Not me! I like company.

The overhead lights go out in the barn at 9 p.m. I wished I'd slept in the farmhouse. I am ashamed to admit it, but I was afraid of the dark.

Eerie shadows leaped and danced on the ceiling and walls of the farrowing barn. I crawled in under a large pillow. Each time I mustered up enough courage to stick my head out to take a peek, I'd see them again. A frightful display of ghostly designs. It gave me the creeps. After all, I'm just a little pig. My eyes were saucer wide. Sleep was impossible.

Gradually, little by little, the patterns went away. As the sows and pigs settled down, so did the patterns.

How foolish I felt when it dawned on me. Dumb me! All that flickering with the lights was nothing more than the big farm hogs and their babies moving around in front of the night lights and heat lamps in their pens.

Good grief! I can't believe I was frightened by a night light. Mama would never find out about that from me!

Finally, the barn was calm and quiet. Everybody slept, except me. I heard every burp and sneeze, every cough and snort the big hogs made. And yet, no sounds, not one came from Sweet Jasmine. Poor thing.

For a few minutes I began to doze, but all too soon I dreamed. Frightening dreams! The ugly, hairless Great Dane dragged me back to the Humane Society by my hind leg. A grayish man with large red eyes met us in the doorway. He was about a foot taller than Kevin Duckworth, the seven foot center on the Oregon Trailblazer's basketball team.

In my dream, the grayish ghost shouted at me. "Now pig! You die!"

Eerie shadows leaped and danced on the
ceiling and walls of the farrowing barn.

He rushed toward me. In his hand was a hypodermic needle pointed in my direction. It was as large as a baseball bat. His big hairy thumb was on the plunger.

He reached out and grabbed me and stuck me in the rump. I screamed, really screamed, for real, and loud, I guess. The screaming didn't wake me up, but the farm hogs snorting for me to "keep quiet" did.

Slowly, I stood up. My legs felt as if they were sinking in sand. I checked my hind end to see if that red eyed monster had really got me. Luckily, it was only a bad dream.

Even when I was wide awake my worst nightmare was that I would wind up back in that Humane Society. Next time, Pam might not be there to save me. I heard Mama say Pam was going away to college. I don't know when.

Sweet Jasmine was not affected by my screams or the loud warnings from the sows. Her silence was a puzzle to me.

The morning sun poked warm rays through the windows and doors.

Arley's son, Joshua, brought breakfast. I heard him talking to Sweet Jasmine.

"Little girl, why are you so quiet? Never a 'hello' nor a 'goodbye' do I get from you."

Sweet Jasmine gave Joshua a pleasant look and continued with breakfast.

A couple of hours later I heard Mama talking to Little Prissy. I was unable to make out their words at this distance. Just the same, by the tone of their voices they were extremely saddened about something.

It was nearly noon before I heard the news. A favorite old tom cat was found dead in the big barn. Mama called him T.C. She said that was short for Tom Cat.

"We buried him in the pet cemetery back in the timber," Mama told me. "We sure loved that cat, Lucy. This place won't seem the same without him. He and Hotsie were Priscilla's best friends." I thought Hotsie was another cat, but Mama explained she was a big Chester White hog.

"I hate to tell the grandkids!" Papa added. "Especially Shawn. He really loved that old cat. In a couple more weeks Tom Cat would have been seventeen years old."

Later, when we were in the farmhouse, I heard Mama tell someone on the phone about the cat's death. Papa had told her the cat just crawled up on a bale of hay and went to his final rest.

As soon as Mama got off the phone, it rang. The ladies who work in the vet's office had a big problem. Some frantic woman had phoned them to say her neighbor had moved away three days ago and left their Pot Bellied pig behind. The lady's kids had coaxed it into their house. Now, the poor thing was having babies on her kitchen floor. The vet was out on call and would not be back in time to help.

"Would Papa like to lend a hand?" the office girl asked.

What a heartless trick, leaving the sow behind, with her babies due any time. How cruel!

Would Papa like to lend a hand? What do you think? Of course. With the address in hand, he skedaddled out the door. The drive took about twenty minutes. The anxious lady waved to him from her front porch.

"Over here," she called.

Papa hurried into the house and there she was, a farrowing sow.

A stereo was blasting from the next room. The sow was terrified. If that wasn't enough to make her nervous, four kids were standing around staring at her.

"Kids, if you have any feelings at all for this frightened little sow, you will turn off that noise, go in the other room and please close the door." Papa said.

"Do it, kids," the woman told them. "Mister, I don't know anything about birthing pigs. I am Cindy Martin." She put out her hand to Papa.

"Hello, Cindy. Everybody calls me Papa. Now, don't you worry. You don't have to know a thing, because I know everything there is to know about birthing pigs, and them some," Papa smiled.

As soon as the room became quiet the little "mother-to-be" began to settle down.

"It's all right, I'm here to help you," Papa spoke softly to the sow.

A black, male pig had been born a few minutes before Papa's arrival. The pig crawled near the sow's belly and was quiet.

The sow was larger than the others Papa had seen. But she was definitely a Pot Belly and had been grossly overfed. At least they hadn't starved her. Papa guessed her weight at about one hundred and twenty-five pounds.

Papa asked for some old towels, warm water, string, sissors and iodine. While Cindy gathered up these things, Papa heard one of the kids say to her, "Mom, are you playing pig nurse?"

Her answer was, "I don't know what I'm doing, Nicholas."

In less than two hours, four healthy babies were nursing their mother. Two boys and two girls.

"What am I going to do?" Mrs. Martin asked Papa. "I have no place to put them. We are just not equipped for pigs, and it's all I can do to keep food on the table for my children."

Papa listened. "You say your neighbors moved away and left her here?"

"They sure did. The whole family moved to Arizona a few days ago. My boy, Mitchell, played with their boys. He said they had been trying to sell her." Cindy admitted she loved animals, but there was no way she could keep these pigs.

"Should I call the Humane Society? Do they take pigs?" she asked.

Papa laughed. "Don't bother calling them. They'd just call me. Tell the kids to come in quietly and have a look. After that, we will load 'em in my little rig and take 'em home. A few more at my place won't matter."

At the supper table, Papa shared the story. He said Cindy Martin certainly looked relieved when he offered to bring the family of pigs home with him.

"That's why I took the covered pickup and two pet porters, just in case. The sow, I've named Ginger. It was all she could do to turn around in the large pet porter. I put her in one and the pigs in the other."

"I'm surprised you didn't bring them right in the house!" Mama teased.

"Maybe tomorrow," Papa chuckled. "Ginger sure liked her apartment. She pigged out on her feed and wanted more. I thought she would never stop drinking water. Those pigs will take some of that excess weight off of her."

"What are you going to do with that collection of Pot Bellied pigs out there?" the vet asked Papa when he called to thank him for helping out.

"Oh, we'll find good homes for them," Papa answered. "But first, we have to train the owners."

I listened when Pot Bellied pigs were discussed. I know they didn't plan on keeping any of us, and why should they? Isn't it enough that they rescue us from death and starvation? We get discarded like an old pair of shoes. They give us a good place to sleep and plenty of good food. Oddly enough, I think they love us all. Maybe I shouldn't, but I love Mama and Papa too. Maybe it wasn't too smart to pretend that this was my forever home. But I did. All I wanted was a good place to be. Was that too much to ask?

Chapter 15.

MAMA AND PAPA MEET FLO

For several days in a row, Flo nosed around in Thomas Creek, asking questions. Today she was at it again. To look at her, you would think she was a Sunday driver, out for a spin. But it wasn't even Sunday. The day was warm, about 75 degrees. Flo had the car windows down, the radio blasting and her blond ringlets bouncing in the breeze.

Feeling hungry, Flo whipped into the parking lot of the local hamburger joint where a lot of friendly locals hung out to catch up on hometown gossip.

Flo placed her order. She collected her drink and sat down at a long table where others were seated.

"Are you new in town or just visiting?" a friendly gentleman asked.

Flo had come to the right place for information. This group knew everything going on in town and a lot that wasn't going on.

Finding me and getting me back was the one thing Flo had on her silly mind. She vowed she would find me and put me up for sale. She wove her clever web of lies.

"Oh, I'm out for a drive. I just wanted to get out and enjoy this beautiful day."

"It is a beautiful day, isn't it? Where do you live?" someone asked her.

"In Salem," Flo answered truthfully.

"In town?"

"Well, in the suburbs," she again answered truthfully. Gosh, two truths in a row. "I was wondering if anyone raised those Pot Bellied pigs to sell over in this area. A friend of mine is shopping for one."

The locals talked it over. A few pets had been seen. All of them knew where the hog farms were, however, nobody had heard of Pot Bellies for sale.

Flo was about to think she had come up empty handed until a toothless, cigar-smoking old man in blue overalls came up with a suggestion.

"Best person to ask is our local vet. He'd know."

Flo smiled sweetly at the fellow. "That is a good idea. I thank you," she told him. But Flo was thinking to herself, "Why didn't I think of that? Why did I have to get the information I need from this disgusting old man!" After that, she wolfed down her lunch. Armed with the address of the Veterinary Clinic, she dashed out the door.

The good folks at the clinic had no way of knowing who Flo was or what she was up to. Flo thought she was being clever. But she was too dumb to be too clever. Did she ever stop to think? No, she did not. Is is possible she could get into trouble for what she was doing? Absolutely!

Yes, the clinic was able to help her. They gave her directions to the farm, Papa's farm. And yes, he had pigs to place in good homes.

I was in the house when Flo drove in. Mama was washing the car. Papa was outside someplace.

I knew trouble was coming. I could feel it in my bones. I had known it for several days. If I had only known Flo was in the area, if only I had been warned of her coming. I could have high-tailed it to the timber and hid out.

Flo had rehearsed over and over her made-up story. She was already in big trouble with her husband and the Humane Society. Now she was getting in deeper and deeper all the time. Flo could get an Academy Award for the act she put on for Papa and Mama.

"Please, please, tell me you are the kind folks caring for my Lucy," she said with the phoniest kind of concern you can imagine.

Mama looked at Flo in disbelief. Who was this person? Was she really Lucy's owner as she claimed?

Papa showed up in time to hear Flo's tall tale.

"I have been worried sick. You do have Lucy, don't you? You did pick her up from the Humane Society?"

Not knowing whether to believe this person or not, Mama and Papa didn't say a word.

"I had to go to Colorado to visit my sick sister. My neighbor was supposed to look after my animals while my husband was away at work. I paid her good money, too. But she left the gate open. Lucy ran into the street and was picked up almost immediately by the dog catcher. I just got home today. You can't imagine how upset I was when I thought Lucy had been put to sleep," Flo lied. "Please tell me you have her and that she is all right, so I can take her home."

Well, you know how kind hearted Mama and Papa are. Flo had convinced them she cared for me and had not been available to pick me up.

"Lucy found a friend at the Humane Society. A young lady who worked a miracle to save Lucy's life. Your pig is a very lucky animal. If she is yours and you want her, I guess you have the right to take her," Papa said. "I must tell you, we have grown fond of her. I'll have to have your name, address and telephone number. The shelter deserves a report of each pig. O.K.?"

"Oh, I'll be glad to give you that information. Anything to get my dear pet back. I'm so glad she is alive."

I get so mad when I think about the dirty trick Flo played on nice folks like Mama and Papa.

While Mama took down the information from Flo, Papa went into the house to get me. He hooked the leash onto my harness kind of sad-like, and led me out to Flo. He never said a word.

The sight of her made me ill. I had known something bad was about to happen, I could feel it coming. Living here on the farm was too good to last. I looked at Mama. She had tears in her eyes.

"Lucy Lo Chow, I hate to see you go, but you belong to this woman and she cares about you," Mama said.

"What in the world did Flo tell them?" I wondered. Whatever it was had convinced them or they would never have let me go. I was unable to speak. A big lump came up in my throat. I was beaten. What could I do? I'm just a pig. Flo didn't even speak to me. Didn't Mama and Papa notice that? She raised the trunk lid, poked me in the pet porter, jumped in her car and drove off with me.

"She didn't bother to say 'Thank you'," Papa said. "After all, we did save Lucy from death."

"And why did she stick her in the trunk?" Mama cried. "Maybe the excitement of having her pet back made her behave strangely," Mama figured. "I'll miss Lucy. We sure got attached to her in a hurry, Papa."

As for me, I felt as if I was being killed off by

inches. First the Humane Society and now this. I was the target of a bad joke, and once again in the hands of this uncaring, crazy person. I was right back where I started.

I could hear Flo laughing madly above the sound of the radio. She feasted on the moment as if she had won the war. What a fruitcake!

She yelled things at me. "I've got you now pig," she cackled, "and I'm keeping you until somebody puts money in my hand to take you away. And then, I'll be rid of you. You won't get away from me this time, pig!"

"Get away? Why didn't I think of that? If I could do it once, I can do it again!" Just for a moment, I felt a glimmer of hope.

But could I escape from Flo's cruelty?

Chapter 16.

THE CLASSIFIED AD

Three weeks had passed since Flo snookered me away from my home on the farm. Flo was a deceitful, conniving witch. I wondered where she hid her broom. Is she the one who rides through the sky on Halloween? "Probably," I decided.

Floyd tried to keep his wife out of trouble, but she paid very little attention to him. He said to her, "Flo, the minute you put an ad in the paper to sell this pig, you'll be in big trouble." Flo's brain does not compute common sense. Not only will she put an ad in the paper, she planned to call in on the Saturday morning classified ads on the local radio station. Floyd had not yet been told about the radio station. Had he known, he'd have had a fit!

I missed Mama and Papa. With them I was somebody special. Besides, it was fun talking to a human.

112

I hoped they missed me too, even if it was just a little bit. Flo's house was filled with contention. I longed for the farm, the rides, the other pigs and all the activity.

And there was a *great deal* of activity back at the farm. I learned about it later. Word got around the community about training pig owners. A couple of newspaper people wrote about it. That brought many families to the farm looking for a pig to own.

Each individual or family received the same treatment. Sometimes Arley's family helped out and enjoyed the fun.

Following a tour of the barn, the prospective owners were escorted into the new orientation room to view two video tapes on the care and feeding of Pot Bellied pigs. One film came by U.P.S. from a breeder in North Carolina. It wasn't bad. The other was homemade. Papa had finally gotten some good use out of the camcorder Deana had given him for Christmas one year. Actually, the tape he put together was pretty good, and funny. There was one shot of his feet. John Henry, one of the barn cats, jumped on Papa's shoulder from the rafters. He startled Papa so much that he nearly dropped his camera. But he did get a good picture of his boots.

Papa's film was all basic stuff. After all he was still learning and had a lot yet to learn. His film included tips on care and feeding, and also pointed out pitfalls to avoid.

Papa was not satisfied with the feed. So far, he had used what was available for miniature pigs from the local feed stores. A poor selection.

"Maybe we'll have to mix our own," he said.

No one was allowed to touch a pig, or even go near one, until he or she had watched both tapes. The kids had to watch too; if they didn't, they couldn't hold a pig. So, they watched. No child was allowed to go wondering around in Papa's barn.

"Kids always unlock my gates. And I am getting too old to go chasing hogs," Papa told the parents.

Next, the family was invited to visit the apartment of the pig of their choice, but only under supervision. Now, each family member knew how to conduct himself. Go in quietly. Find a place to sit, usually the floor, and why not, it was clean carpet. Only one person at a time should call to the pig. Don't reach out too quickly or make sudden moves. If you do, the pig will go the other way. Give it some time. Let the pig warm up to you. When it comes near enough, reach out and offer a one-finger scratch behind the ear, at first. After that first touch, the pig will usually let you pet him, scratch his back and rub his tummy. All pigs love tummy rubs. As soon as one trusts you enough to let you do it, it will fall right over on its side and beg for more.

One by one, each family member must go through

this same procedure. Sometimes the bonding between a pig and a family happens quickly, sometimes slowly and sometimes, never. Or, a pig may dislike one member of the family, for no apparent reason.

When I don't like somebody, I let them know it right away. First, I shake my head fast in both directions, trying to scare them off. If I need to be more agressive, I whack them with the side of my head. If that doesn't work I lunge in their direction and bite at them. At the same time I make a deep throated woofing sound. The last resort is to bite. I have never had to do that. Yuck! I might get sick. I hope I never have to bite anybody. I couldn't even bite Flo, although she certainly deserved it.

Papa wrote to a Pot Bellied pig registry out of state. He read one of their advertisements stating how they would be happy to answer any question one might have. Papa asked them about feeding, what to feed etc. They didn't even answer his letter. Papa was put out about it.

He said, "If I had some good information about these pigs I would share it." And he would, too.

Papa said if he could find a breeder whose pigs all looked good and were contented, he would pick his brain and copy his feeding program. He found such a place in Hubbard, at Diane Waggerby's. Only it was a her. What a delightful soul. She loved every pig in her barn and she had lots of Pot Bellied pigs to love.

Sonny and Cher

There was even a Sonny and Cher, brother and sister. He was all white and she was black. Cher was running around in the barn visiting with each pen as she passed.

There was a grand champion sow in the lot, which came as no surprise. Every pig in the place looked great! Gentle and friendly and well formed. Even their hide and hair was shiny and healthy looking.

No doubt about it, Papa was glad he had made this trip to Hubbard. He asked a million questions and made a friend. Truth of the matter is, Diane was as particular as Papa. She had run across a pig feed that she swore by. Strangely enough, when Papa checked the formula, it practically matched up with the one he had written down on paper, the one he was trying to find.

"Well I'll be jiggered!" Papa grinned as he read the formula. "And to think someone makes it." Papa bought some of Diane's feed until he could get more of his own.

Papa is as good as his word. He wrote to the company and asked permission to share this Pot Bellied pig formula with everybody. He said to tell you, this is not a paid commercial. In the back of the book, you will find this information. Papa likes to feed the best. He believes this feed is the best now available.

Many time after that Papa and Mama visited other breeders and owners of Pot Bellied pigs, but never,

ever did they find the same quality as those pigs they had seen in Hubbard. Mama said that place even had two bath tubs and a rocking chair.

Usually, Mama and Papa did their visiting in the evenings, unless the Portland Trail Blazer's basketball team had a televised game that night. They sure got loud when they watched those games. I never saw them get quite so excited about anything else, especially Mama.

"Way to go Terry, another great three pointer," they'd yell for Terry Porter, or "Wow, did you see that shot Clyde Drexler made? Wasn't that terrific!" Silly questions, they were both glued to the television. Then sometimes Papa would get mad at the referees. "A foul? That was a flagrant foul against Kersey!" And so it went. All that yelling hurt my ears. I'd find a quiet spot a couple of rooms away.

But when the game was at half-time, they both headed for the kitchen and of course I followed. Mama made popcorn while Papa opened a couple of cans of pop. I hung around for anything that dropped on the floor. I never did find out what that pop tasted like. Mama said it wasn't good for pigs. It must have been good for humans. I heard those pop tops popping a lot. But popcorn, Mama never had to vacuum any off the floor. I was always glad when they missed their mouths. I liked it when kids were there eating. They were always dropping food. Mama said I was a regular little vacuum sweeper.

Living at Flo's I liked thinking about living back at the farm. It took my mind off all the chaotic confusion brought about by Mrs. Giddyhead herself. There was no peace in this house.

Flo wanted to be at home when the phone calls began coming in from her ad. She told Floyd not to expect her to go anyplace with him for awhile. According to her, a million people would be coming to see me, but it didn't happen. The first day the phone did not ring. The second day, two people called for information. Do they make good pets? Can you housebreak one? What do they eat, etc.?

Flo began talking to herself, "I am so tired of answering questions. I want money, money, that's what I want!"

Can you imagine Flo telling anyone how to take care of a pig when she doesn't even know herself? I knew I would end up back in the Humane Society for sure.

All the time, she was telling callers what great pets pigs are. Then why was she trying to sell me. What a hypocrite!

Saturday morning Mama spotted Flo's telephone number in the "Pigs For Sale" ads. It was also Saturday morning when Mrs. Bates heard Flo advertising a pig for sale on the radio classified ads. She almost choked on her Armour Star bacon when she heard

Flo describing me as the pig she had for sale.

"That woman!" Mrs. Bates yelled at her husband, "that horrible, conniving woman has somehow stolen Lucy back and is trying to sell her. I have to call the farm in Thomas Creek, right away,"

Now it was Mrs. Bate's turn to talk to herself. She was fuming mad.

Mama and Papa felt foolish when they learned how they had been stonewalled by sweet-talking Flo. She had lied to them about being out of town. She had lied to them about everything.

I'll bet a dollar to a pile of pig manure that she doesn't even have a sister in Colorado. And if she does, she probably doesn't claim Flo," Papa said.

"She is in a lot of trouble," Mrs. Bates told Mama. "When she failed to pick up Lucy at the shelter in the allotted time she gave up her rights to her pet. Things might be different if she truly was out of town, but she was here all the time. She lied. She knew we had the pig. Animal control had already talked to her neighbors."

At that time, I didn't know what was going on with Mama, Mrs. Bates and all that. I only knew that at any moment I could be sold to God knows who. I had something else on my mind. Running away! Back to the farm. Trouble was, I didn't know the way, for sure.

Mrs. Bates said she would handle Flo Fevers.

Mama and Papa had enough to do now without having to worry about her.

Guess what? Sweet Jasmine sure enough was deaf. Which means she couldn't hear, neither could she speak much. Occassionally she grunted a strange sounding grunt, probably because she didn't know what a grunt was supposed to sound like, never having heard one.

Word got around about Sweet Jasmine and her problem. One day a young married couple drove out from Albany to see her. You know what? They couldn't hear or speak either.

Right away, Papa and Mama liked them. The couple, James and Jenny Hunter, spoke to each other in sign language, really fast. Mama wished she had taken those sign language classes when they had been offered at church. But it worked out all right. By the use of gestures and a pad and pencil they were able to communicate.

The Hunters watched the video tapes. Papa wrote down the things that were necessary for them to hear.

"Oh Papa, I sure hope Sweet Jasmine and this couple take to each other," Mama said.

Mama did not know that Jenny could read lips. Jenny handed Mama a note that read, "I hope so too."

The Hunters stayed in Jasmine's apartment all morning. Before they left, James penciled Papa a

note. "We will be back tomorrow. O.K.?" Papa
smiled and nodded, yes.

Sure enough, the next morning James and Jenny
returned, eager to see little Jasmine. The pig greated
them with great enthusiasm. She jumped up on the
gate wanting them to pet her. Again, they stayed the
morning. About eleven a.m. Mama showed up with a
pitcher of pop and two glasses. In her apron pocket
she carried Cheerios for the pigs. She gave James and
Jenny a handful to feed to Jasmine. Cheerios are
great snacks for Pot Bellies. Sweets are out.

"I've never seen a pig bond with strangers as
quickly as Jasmine did to that sweet young couple. I
believe they were meant for each other," Papa said.
"I sure hope it works out."

Once again, the following morning, they returned
with a lengthy note. The note was written with great
affection, saying simply how they had fallen in love
with Sweet Jasmine and how much they wanted her
for their very own.

"If you tell us we can have her, today we will
shop for everything required to care for her the way
the video tape explained: a pet porter, blankets, food,
vitamins, coat care oil, etc.," the note stated.

Papa read the note while they played with Sweet
Jasmine. He smiled at them and nodded, yes. They
hugged each other and mouthed "thank you so
much" to Papa.

All pigs should have it so lucky, huh?

Back at Flo's the phone calls had not yet produced a buyer. She was as wild as a caged squirrel.

When I first got back to Flo's she watched me every minute. She thought I'd run off. Then I learned to pretend. I pretended to be content and she forgot to watch.

I had plans. I was sure I could find my way to the farm. Well, almost sure. I had another worry, ---What if the dog catcher captured me again?

Chapter 17.

THE CITY COUNCIL

The pet owner's training program got more attention. Even the city council in Thomas Creek had temporarily overturned their rule of "no pigs for pets in the city limits". A couple of families had challenged the ruling. The new rule was a little better. Now, the owner had to attend training classes like the ones held on the farm.

The city council members looked out of place strolling through the farrowing barn. But you have to give them credit. At least they were willing, at Papa's invitation, to come out and see the difference between farm hogs and miniature Pot Bellied pigs.

Some city fathers class Pot Bellied pigs as farm animals. That's the excuse they use for not permitting them in the city limits. Mama said you can't expect these city folks to know everything, although some of them act like they do. She also said with all the magazines and newspaper articles about Pot Bellied pigs in the past few months they should know a lot more than they do, that is of course if they can read.

Papa stood right up in City Council Meeting and spoke up for pigs. Mama thought he did a good job.

He said, "Farm hogs are raised for meat on the table. Just name one person in the United States of America who has ever eaten a Pot Bellied pig pork chop. It just doesn't happen, fellows. I'm sorry, but you don't have the slightest idea what you are talking about. If you really want to be a servant to the community, I believe that's what your campaigning was all about, then I invite you out to the farm. We have both kinds of hogs in the same building. Unless you are blind, if shouldn't take you too long to figure out the difference between a farm hog and a pet."

So now, here they were. Papa introduced his guests to the farm hogs first. The adult sows weigh from three hundred to about eight hundred pounds. He tarried longer in front of the older, larger sows to make his point.

"These hogs have been with us all their lives. They were born here, in this barn. You can see by their size no one in his right mind would bring one in the house for a pet. These hogs, gentlemen, are farm hogs. By the time these sows are a year old they've had a litter of pigs and are at least two hundred and fifty pounds." Papa looked squarely at his guests.

"Now come on down the hallway with me and I will show you some little pigs who are wrongfully classed as farm animals." Papa was in control and enjoying every minute of it as he lead the small parade of men down the hallway.

Mama was showing the Conover family the little sow who had had her babies in the neighbor's kitchen floor. Papa had renamed the sow "Tramp".

"Well, I still say a pig is a pig," Horace Hunsaker remarked to the other councilmen.

"And, a cat is a cat, even if it is a tiger. Wouldn't you agree with that, fellows?" Papa grinned.

Hunsaker squinted up his eyes and shot a dirty look toward Papa who had now reached the orientation room.

"If you were in the market for a pet pig, I would have to insist we stop here to look at two films. Between the two of them you would learn the basics of caring for and feeding a pet pig," Papa told them.

Now they were in front of Tramp's apartment. She and her babies were real charmers. One was half buried under a sofa pillow on the little red, short legged couch. Another stood quietly by its mother. The Conover children were petting the other two and the pigs were enjoying it.

Tramp had slimmed down quite a lot. She was about the size of a medium sized, short legged dog.

"These pens look better than some homes I've

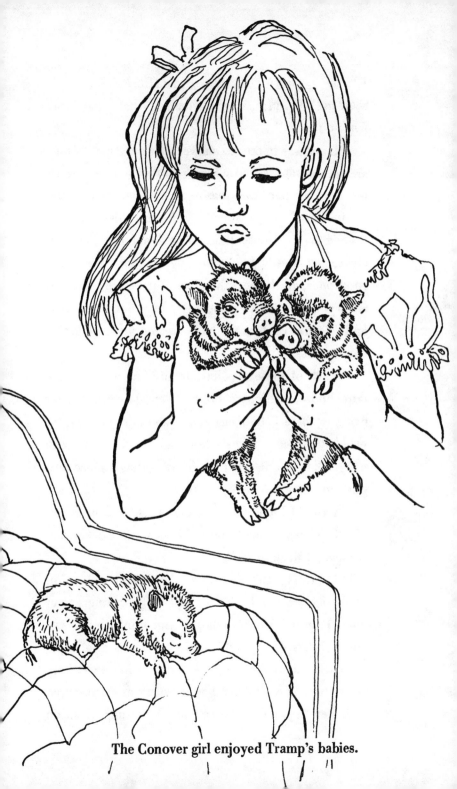

The Conover girl enjoyed Tramp's babies.

been in," Mr. Morgan exclaimed. "What's the deal? Why so fancy?"

Mama was happy to answer that question. "These are house pets, Mr. Morgan. You don't raise a house pet in a hog pen. The reason many of these pets end up in the Humane Society is because they weren't trained to be house pets. Papa and I are trying to change all that. I know the big breeders, the really good ones, do the best they can. But we are small and are trying to set an example. We only have a few pigs and because of that we have created a near Utopian situation."

"Each of these pigs has already had a turn in the farm house, without a hitch," Papa bragged. "After living in these little apartments the house presents no problem. It only takes a few minutes to housebreak a pig. That's done out here by providing a place outside, one they can easily get to."

"I wish I knew your secret," Carl Gortner laughed. "I've been trying to housebreak a new Cocker pup for several weeks now."

"I hate to tell you this, Carl," Papa told him, "but pigs are much cleaner and faster learners than dogs. I know! We have both. And think about this, fellows. Pigs don't bark! Did you ever hear of a pig disturbing someone's night's sleep? It has never happened here and we have had as many as six hundred hogs here at one time. And another thing, dogs do their business all over your yard. A pig will go in the same spot, every time. They don't shed. They have no fleas. What does that tell you?"

"And they don't smell bad like dogs and other animals," Mama added. "There is no bad odor about a pig. That probably surprises you."

"What?" Hunsaker didn't believe her.

Mama told him how it is. "Well, the only time a hog smells is when the farmer is too lazy to clean the pens."

"I've noticed how fresh this barn smells," one of the councilmen said. "I recognize the scent of cedar shavings and clean wheat straw."

"So did I," another added.

"We are using a new feed that provides added benefits, a feed prepared for Pot Bellied pigs. The pigs get more complete digestion of protein, which means less odor in the manure."

The Conovers had been listening, but it was time for them to go home. Papa asked if there were any other members of their family.

"Yes, our boy Billy is nine. He is in school."

"Next time, bring the boy. We will have to see if he bonds with the pig before you can take it home. He will also have to view the tapes."

"But we have already viewed the tapes, we can tell our son," Mrs. Conover told Papa.

"I'm sorry, maybe you could, but that's not the

way it works," Papa replied. "We have to be sure the boy and the pig like each other. If they don't, you'll all be miserable."

"All right," Mrs. Conover agreed. "I'm sure you folks know best."

The pigs were not for sale. They were for placement in good homes. Every precaution was taken for the safety of the animal.

When the Conovers had gone, Mr. Hunsaker made a bad mistake.

"Why are you so particular?" he asked. "They are only hogs."

"Only hogs, huh?" Papa said calmly. "Well sir, hogs don't get out of the yard and bite little children. What was that I read in the paper about your Pit Bull?"

Hunsaker's face turned bright red. Papa had settled the score. Nobody cracks ugly remarks about pigs around Papa and gets away with it, nobody!

Five of the six councilmen were glad they had taken the time to find out about pigs like me. Three of them actually expressed an interest in having a pig for a pet.

James and Jenny Hunter live in Thomas Creek. Papa wondered if Hunsaker would try to stop them from having Sweet Jasmine in town. Wouldn't that be a shame? Time will tell!

Chapter 18.

DUMPSTER

I n the early afternoon, someone from the vet's office called. Nobody was in the farm house. Mama and Papa had gone to Salem to shop and to visit their daughter.

Jacob let the phone ring several times before he picked up the extension in the farrowing barn. He wrote a message for Mama and Papa to call the vet as soon as possible.

Late that afternoon Mama returned the call. The vet needed some help. Some cruel individual had thrown a pig in a rubbish bin and left it there to die. Boy! Mama was outraged.

"Who would do such a thing?" Mama grumbled to herself as she searched the barns for Papa to tell him the news.

They lost no time getting into town.

When Mama saw the pig, there in the vet's office,

she could not hold back the tears. The pig looked like death warmed over. Dr. Mike had set the hind leg and wrote "Dumpster" on the cast. Mike's wife thought Dumpster was a terrible name for a little girl pig. But Dr. Mike thought it fit. You may think so too when you hear the story. Even though Dumpster had been treated, she was still seriously ill and as Dr. Mike said, "She is not out of the woods". Which meant she could die. It was pneumonia. There was cotton and alcohol by the pig. Someone had given her an alcohol bath. That helps to bring down the fever.

"What happened?" Papa asked. "Who's pig is she, Mike?"

"All I know is, while Allen Hopkins was making a trash pick up behind North's Hardware he heard a sound coming from inside the big blue dumpster. He said if he hadn't shut down his truck to have some lunch he wouldn't have heard it. Way down in a wet corner, under all the empty boxes and trash, he found this shivering little Pot Bellied pig with a broken leg. Not knowing what else to do, he called the Police Station," Dr. Mike explained.

"Officer Ben Parker came and put the pig in his patrol car on an old shirt. He said it was the nearest dead thing he'd ever seen.

"Anyway, he brought it over here to us. I shot it full of antibiotics and some pain killer and set the leg. Actually, right now she's coming along a lot better

than we had hoped for. Looks to me like the pig had
been pretty well taken care of until it fell on hard
times. Probably been in the dumpster for a couple of
days. But the cool nights and lying in that water
didn't help any."

"So, you think it will live?" Mama asked.

"With good care and vittles," the vet smiled.

Now Papa knew why they were called in. "That's
where we come in, Mama."

No one had any idea where the pig had come
from. What the vet did know, was that two families in
Thomas Creek had pet pigs. Each had felt the wrath
of the city council, especially the wrath of council-
man Horace Hunsaker.

One pig lived with Wes Beckstead, his wife and
eleven children. They loved their sixty pound, fully
grown, white "Princess". She's too fat, but well cared
for. They live out on the curve toward West Thomas
Creek.

John and Lula Potter owned the other one. Their
house is not more than a block back of North's Hardware. Potters always have lots of pets for their son
Andrew, who is afflicted with Down's syndrome. The
vet said he heard Andrew had a pig but he had not
seen it.

Papa remembered Hunsaker making a distasteful
remark about the Potter kid having a pig. When Papa
learned the boy was retarded, he thought badly of

Hunsaker for saying such a thing. Actually, Hunsakers and Potters live in the same block.

"Do you want us to take Dumpster now?" Mama asked Dr. Mike.

"You probably could, but her lungs aren't clear yet."

"When you are ready for us, give us a call," Mama told him. "We have quite a few already. You should have one for a pet, Mike," Mama smiled. She knew he loved all kinds of animals.

"Mama, everybody doesn't take to pigs like we do," Papa reminded her.

"Well, it wouldn't be too difficult to become attached to Dumpster," Mike told them.

"When we get her well she will be needing a good home, you know. I don't suppose we'll ever know who the owner is. Nobody will ever admit to tossing a pet in a trash bin," Mama said.

"The police already have an idea what happened, but they aren't saying anything," Mike said.

What about the person who threw that pig in the trash? If the pig died could that person be charged with murder? And if not, why not?

Who did throw that pig in the dumpster and what will happen to him?

Chapter 19.

BAD LUCK FOR LUCY

Floyd told Brian he had telephoned several people selling Pot Bellied pigs. The going price is $250.00 and less. Flo continued to hold out for $750.00 for me. There were no takers and she was angry, really angry. Every day Flo got a little wilder. Her fits of temper were scary. Putting up with dog and cat food had been necessary to stay alive. But lately, I got very little to no food at all. This morning she had put down dry cat food for me. Just a little. Not enough to stuff a dead mouse. I ran to eat it before the dog got there, but before I got to it, Flo gave the dish a kick across the kitchen. I didn't get a bite. Flo laughed one of her savage laughs. Was she going berserk?

I ran to get away from her. That enraged her. She ran after me with an iron skillet. Just as she let it fly I darted under the couch. Old Gus, the bulldog, tried to protect me by growling at her. Then she got angry at Gus.

When she threw the skillet, bacon grease flew all over that yellow velvet couch of hers. I got blamed for that. I waited until she was busy cleaning up before I ran to the bedroom and hid behind the headboard.

I had to get away from her before she either starved me to death or killed me. As crazy as she was acting I was afraid to go near her.

Brian was nice to me when Flo was out of sight but seldom was he there.

Every day I watched for someone to leave the front gate open. But no one did. If I were left out long enough I could root a tunnel under the fence and escape. Flo was watching me again. Not only was the gate closed, Flo had Floyd put a tight spring on it. Now the gate had to be held open to pass through. I could escape only when someone was coming in or out. But so far, I missed out, every time

"If I don't get something to eat soon I won't have enough energy to run away," I told myself.

The next few days that followed were unbearable. That woman yelled and screamed at me all the time. Floyd told her to stop it, but she never listened. I thought maybe Floyd would feed me, but he didn't. One day Flo put a rotten apple and some molded bread on the floor and expected me to pig it down.

As hungry as I was, I was too smart for that.

She screeched, "Eat it or starve, pig. That's all you'll get from me." True enough. No more food came my way, all day. The next morning Brian was there for breakfast. He slipped me a piece of French toast and a big handful of grapes. That night, he sneaked me some leftovers. Between Brian's visits I got pretty hungry. How could Flo expect to sell a starving pig?

Mrs. Bates had been taking care of business. Remember Wrinkle, the pig who died in my pen in the shelter? Well, Cory got drunk and bragged to someone about giving the family's pet pig a good taste of his boot before tying it to a tree at the Humane Society. The "Someone" was an animal lover. He reported Cory to the shelter. Cory was assessed a big fine. Boy! Was he angry! Facing his family after they found out what he had done wasn't too much fun for him either.

At least Cory had been punished. The case against Flo Fevers was more complicated. The neighbors on Bodger Avenue all knew about Flo. Gail Snoopy liked me. Gail talked to a few of the people in the block about filing a complaint against Flo. Gail was elected to file the complaint. She admitted she wanted to be the one who did it, anyway.

When word of the neighborhood action reached Mrs. Bates, she was overjoyed. That was the ammunition she needed to stop Flo Fevers. Now there were cruelty to animal charges on top of everything else.

But first Mrs. Bates had to get me out of that house.

She called Mama and Papa to bring them up to date on me and on Flo Fevers. Mama and Papa blamed themselves. To hear I was being mistreated did not set well with them. Yes, they would be glad to testify in court and they hoped that day would come soon.

The barn had been a place of excitement and activity. Lots of pigs, and families who wanted one. Dumpster was still in the farm house and would remain there until the cast came off her leg. She was a very loving pig, but so sad, as if she had lost her best friend. Perhaps she had. Mama told me later that Dumpster learned to slide down the back porch slide on three feet. I guess it was pretty funny to watch.

Tramp and her four babies had gone to good homes. In fact, Tramp and her smallest pig went to the same family. While choosing a pig the Cereghinos confessed their entire family had a soft spot in their hearts for Tramp. Tramp knew it and responded with pure affection.

James and Jenny Hunter, the deaf couple, truly believed a miracle had come their way in the form of a deaf pig, Sweet Jasmine. Do you suppose Sweet Jasmine will be able to read sign language? Who knows? Wouldn't that be wonderful?

With fewer pigs to care for, at present, Papa and Mama decided to go and listen in on the Thomas Creek City Council Meeting. Pot Bellied pigs might just be on the agenda.

They weren't a bit surprised to find it was Hunsaker causing all the trouble. The man hated pigs. He said he had heard more complaints from citizens about pigs living within the city limits. When he was asked who made the complaints, he did not reply.

"I make a motion we reconsider our last ruling and make it illegal for anyone to keep a pig for a pet within the city limits. Let's have a unanimous vote on this."

No one seconded his motion. Since no one did, the motion failed. The mayor dropped the subject and began talking about a new air conditioning system for the Police Station.

Hunsaker was furious. He sat there, red in the face and downed a couple of glasses of water from his pitcher. He glared at Papa, who was grinning broadly.

Papa and Mama didn't stay for the entire meeting. Before leaving town they stopped at Bailey's Ice Cream Parlor for a treat. They sat with the Greystones, their former neighbors who once owned Piston, when he was a troublesome burro. They were back in town to visit their son.

Mama ordered a hot fudge sundae and Papa pigged out on a mile-high ice cream cone.

Dr. Mike came in. He told Papa to stop by the Police Station on his way home and talk to officer Ben Parker.

"Why?" Papa wondered, on the way to the Police Station. "Maybe Hunsaker wants me put in jail for raising Pot Bellied pigs in the country," Papa laughed.

"It's about Dumpster." Mama guessed. "Maybe that notice in the paper did some good." The police had asked for anyone having any information about the Pot Bellied pig found in the dumpster behind North's Hardware to please come forward.

Mama was right. It was about Dumpster. Ben Parker told them that Mary Curry's ten year old boy, Charlie, had seen it all. His story fit with the vet's report.

"We believe the pig to be the Potter boy's pet. I called on them the day after the pig's discovery in the trash bin. They had a pig all right, but thought someone had stolen it out of the back yard. That was three days before the pig in the trash bin turned up. The Potters had taken Andrew to Salem for his classes. When they returned home their pig was gone. I guess the boy really loved that pig. But old Hunsaker had been over to their house a couple of times, raising the devil about it. They were afraid to report it stolen. That's all I can tell you folks right now, but I'll be out to see you tomorrow afternoon. I thought that pig died. The vet tells me it is doing fine," Officer

Parker concluded his story.

"You have made me curious," Mama grinned, "but I won't ask any more questions. Can you tell us more tomorrow?"

"Yes, by tomorrow, I can," he answered.

All the next morning Papa and Mama tried to guess and speculate, speculate and guess.

"Sorry, folks, I didn't mean to sound so secretive last night," Officer Parker told them when he arrived. "Animal control had to do their job before I could say much."

"Well, we are anxious to hear what you have to tell us. Does the pig really belong to Andrew Potter?" Mama asked.

"I am pretty sure it does. We will know when the Potters can identify the pig," he answered.

"The vet brought us a report after he set the pig's leg. The break was caused by a dog bite, a strong dog's bite. Charlie Curry saw Hunsaker's Pit Bull in Potter's back yard. The boy was riding his bike around over there. He hurried to Hunsaker's, a few doors away and told them where their dog was. By the time Hunsaker got to the Potter's yard, the pig looked dead, but that dog was still dragging it by a hind leg. Hunsaker yelled for his dog to get home. Charlie said he pretended to leave but rode around the back of Lacy's garage and watched. He said Hunsaker looked around to see if anybody was watching. When he thought no one was, he tossed the pig in the trash bin.''

"Oh my! I knew there was something about that man I didn't like," Papa said angrily.

Mama agreed. "That boy, Charlie, it took courage for him to tell on Hunsaker. What about Potters? When can we expect them?"

"Any time that is good for you folks," Ben answered.

"I don't think we should wait another minute," Mama said.

Ben called the Potters from the kitchen phone. As he left the farm, the Potters drove in the driveway. Andrew had not been told about the pig. When his parents were sure it was his pet, they would tell him.

As soon as the pig heard John and Lula Potter's voices at the door she raced toward them. The cast on her leg had not slowed her down. Neither John nor Lula could hold back the tears.

"Oh Funny Face, you are alive," Lula sputtered, wiping her eyes.

Seeing the pig, John hurried out to the car to fetch Andrew. The boy was thirteen years old.

"She's alive, Andrew. Funny Face is alive. She was hurt by a dog. You'll see a cast on her leg, but the cast is helping her broken leg to heal. These kind folks have been taking care of her." John told his son.

Andrew became very excited. He ran to the

house. Papa swung the door open.

"Come on in here, young man, and claim this pig," Papa grinned.

Andrew fell to his knees to hug his pig. It was hard to tell who was the happiest. Mama wiped her eyes on her apron. She told me later, it was a grand sight to see.

"So you are the one she misses?" Mama said to Andrew.

"He loves that pig," Lula Potter told Mama. "How can we repay you for taking care of our Funny Face?"

"Seeing a happy kid reunited with his pet is all the payment Mama and I will ever need," Papa replied.

"I sure like her name Funny Face better than Dumpster," Papa told Andrew.

"Dumpster? Yuck! That's a bad name," Andrew replied. Everybody laughed.

Mama and Papa were happy they had been privileged to care for Andrew's pig.

"I've never seen a pig as attached to a boy as that one is to Andrew," she said. "And to think he almost lost her."

A happy ending for Andrew and Dumpster, I mean Funny Face. But what about me, Lucy Lo Chow? Flo still had control and she was slowly starving me to death.

Would I ever see Papa and Mama again?

Andrew and Dumpster are reunited.

Chapter 20

LUCY LO CHOW

For five days I had not had a mouthful of food. Brian had not been around. He called Floyd with news of an emergency. His mother ran a butcher knife through her hand while trying to separate two frozen hamburger patties. He must take her to a specialist in Seattle for surgery. I was sorry to hear about his mother, but that meant I wouldn't eat again that day.

All morning I kept to myself under the desk. I asked myself, "Why is this happening to me? Do I deserve such cruel treatment?" My stomach hurt. Sometimes I shook. Each day my body grew weaker and weaker. There was no escape. I cried and cried and wanted Mama and Papa.

Oh, I wish, I wish, I was granted just one wish. I would turn into a human. A large human. I'd put Flo in a cage. I'd yell and scream at her, let her out and throw a skillet at her. I'd tell her how much I hated her, as she tells me. I'd prepare a plate of her favorite food and throw it on the floor for old Gus and then, I would laugh, ha,ha,ha! But, could I? Could I be so cruel?

I cried some more. The cat felt sorry for me. She came near me and purred. But the cat didn't like me well enough to share her food. I'd hate to be a cat. They eat mice guts! Yuck!

Suddenly, the door bell rang. From under the desk, I could not see the door. I heard a man's voice. I heard him say something to Flo about a Pot Bellied pig. She said she did not own one. How peculiar. Wasn't she trying to sell me and get me out of her sight? Maybe he wanted to buy me.

I was determined to make it to the hallway, even if it took all my strength. I had to see who was there. It was a bald man in a greenish uniform. I had seen this man before. He spotted me.

"I thought you said you didn't own a pig, Mrs. Fevers. What is that, a hippopotamus?" the man asked.

Flo was caught in another lie.

"I have an order to pick up your pig, and by the looks of the poor thing I should have been here a week ago."

Floyd arrived home in his pickup truck. He noticed the man in the doorway and the County Animal

Control vehicle parked in front of the house. Across the street, neighbors stood together in small groups and gawked, and snickered.

"He's going to take the pig," Flo shouted at her husband. "Stop him."

"What is your problem, Flo? You don't want the poor thing. You've starving it to death just because nobody will pay the ungodly high price you want for it. I'm tired of you taking out your stupidity on this animal. Now, pick up that pig and give it to this fellow," Floyd was shouting.

"But Floyd!" she protested.

"Don't, 'But Floyd' me. If you ever bring another pig home to mistreat, I'll toss you and the pig out. Do you hear me?" Floyd got louder.

I was enjoying every minute of it. I think the man in the green suit was, too. Now, I remembered. He was from the Humane Society. He was in and out of the place all the time.

Somehow I did not care. Go ahead, take me back to that barking bastion. Let me be put down by lethal injection or whatever they do to unwanted pets like me. I would rather be dead than hungry and hated.

I bawled all the way to the shelter. This time there were no other stops. I was all alone.

All too soon I stood in a familiar pen. Wrinkle had died here, right before my eyes, in this very pen.

Several workers from the shelter came by and

stared at me. Pam, who had rescued me on my first visit, was not among them. I had no hope of being saved this time.

"She is so thin," someone said, and all agreed. "This pig's feeding time is right now. I'll get her some pellets and see if I can scrounge up some fruit or something."

"Why?" I questioned. "I might as well die hungry. What difference does it make now?" Even so, their kindness was appreciated and I did enjoy the food. It was wonderful.

As usual the barking thundered through the building, loud and deafening. For some reason I was able to tune it out. Perhaps it was because I had accepted my fate. Three days would pass away, and so would I. No more tears. My belly was full. I chose a spot on the cement floor and slept. And slept. At feeding time in the late afternoon more delicious food was given to me with caring hands. The fellow who brought it even called me Lucy Lo Chow, the name Mama had given to me. I wondered how he knew.

I went back to sleep. Once in the night when I woke up, I discovered a large, pink blanket folded under me. Who had shown me such kindness? Someone nice.

Not long after breakfast I was carried from my pen to the main entry area.

"Has it been three days already?" I asked myself.

I would rather be dead than hungry and hated.

"Have I lost all sense of time?" The kind attendant took me to the sun porch where I had first met Mama and Papa. I wondered why. When she opened the door I became more confused and surprised.

I didn't feel much like smiling, but everybody in the room was smiling at me. Gail Snooky and her twins were there. So was Alice Bennington, and several other people from the neighborhood. The fellow in the green uniform was there, and Mrs. Bates. And then I saw Mama and Papa, both wearing big smiles.

Mama came and took me from the worker.

"Dear little girl, I am so glad to see you. Can you ever forgive us for letting that person take you away from us?"

I did not know what to say. What did it all mean.

"She is all yours, again!" Mrs. Bates said happily. She handed Papa my adoption papers. "You won't have to worry about Flo Fevers ever again. We will handle her in court. I think her husband finally put the fear of God into her."

"Nobody is ever gonna get this pig," Mama said happily. "She is ours forever. Right, Papa?"

"Right!" he agreed. "If it's all right with you, Lucy. We sure missed you."

I was in the state of shock. It was too good to be true.

Mrs. Bates brought cookies and lemonade for the

occasion.

One minute I think I'm going to die. The next minute I'm in heaven. But this is the kind of heaven I like. The other kind can wait. It took me a while to realize that everything was O.K. I was so happy I could shout. I'm safe. Mama and Papa want me. I'm not unwanted anymore.

I rode to the farm on Mama's lap. She said I was as light as a feather. We talked a little. Everything had happened so fast. I mostly listened.

All the Pot Bellies had been placed. I would be the only one, for now.

Papa said they would have me back in shape in no time at all. I believed him. At the farm, there was plenty of the right kind of food and care.

A few days later Papa read something aloud from the County Courier that made me fall on the floor and laugh. Flo Fevers had been fined $750.00. It was the *amount* that made me laugh. The court released her to the custody of her husband.

I heard Mama say that Horace Hunsaker got what was coming to him too. He was given a stiff fine, kicked off the city council and had to pay the vet bill for Dumpster. And there's more. He was ordered to have that Pit Bull put down before it hurt someone else. There is yet more. All the good folks in Thomas Creek are urging the Potters to sue Hunsaker for the stress he put upon Andrew. Papa thought that was a good idea too.

The kitchen phone rang. Papa did the listening.

"We've got to go to Salem," he said when he had finished listening. "A security guard heard a pig in the trunk of a car in the bank parking lot. He reported it to the police. The pig belonged to a young lady who worked in the bank. Her apartment owner would not permit her to leave the pig home alone all day in the apartment, so she left it in the trunk of her car. It's a wonder it didn't die in there. When she realized she had no other choice, she gave it to the shelter."

"Let's go get it," Mama smiled.

"Me too!" I added.

And we are all living happily on the farm, ever after.

The End.

POT BELLIED PIG FEED
By Colene Copeland

My husband, Bob, and I would like to share with you what we believe to be the best Pot Bellied pig feed on the market today. (10 August 1993) The man who developed this formula is Jim Zamzow.

This is not a paid advertisement. It is our personal opinion and personal preference of feed after trying numerous brands that just did not do the job.

Jim says this. "Pot bellied pigs should not be fed conventional pig food for the following reasons. Pot bellied pigs are vegetarians and commercial pig feed contains meat products. Regular pig feed is designed to quickly increase weight and muscle with no concern for life expectancy. My formula will result in better health and longer life span through the use of all-vegetable proteins, amino acid chelated minerals and digestive aids.

Made from chemical free grain, this feed is the state of the art ration for Pot Bellied pigs. More complete digestion of protein means less stool odor and improved feed utilization means less stool volume, making my formula ideal for healthier pets."

For further information write or telephone:
Dynamite Specialty Products
220 Reynolds Lane
P.O. Box 777
Selah, Wa. 98942
(509) 697-4647

DYNAMITE™ MINIATURE PIG FEED
for Pot Bellied Pigs

INGREDIENTS:
Ground Corn, Ground Barley, Ground Wheat, Ground Oats, Whole Extruded Soybeans, Corn Germ Meal, Linseed Meal, Dicalcium Phosphate, Calcium Carbonate, Salt, Vitamin A Supplement, D-Activated Animal Sterol (source of Vitamin D3), Riboflavin Supplement, Niacin Supplement, Calcium Pantothenate, Choline Chloride, Vitamin B12 Supplement, Iron Carbonate, Zinc Oxide, Manganous Oxide, Copper Oxide, Cobalt Carbonate, Calcium Iodate, Red Iron Oxide, Chelates of Iron, Zinc, Manganese, Magnesium, Copper and Cobalt.

DIRECTIONS:
Babies: ¼ cup twice daily.
Youth (20-30 lb pigs): ½ cup twice daily.
Adult: ¾ - 1 cup twice daily.
Active, Energetic Adult (trouble keeping weight on):
  up to 2 cups daily.

GUARANTEED ANALYSIS:

Crude Protein, not less than 12.00%
Crude Fat, not less than 2.50%
Crude Fiber, not more than 8.00%

**This company also provides suppliments for pregnant and lactating sows and juvenile pigs. You may want to inquire about these products.

GUARANTEED VITAMIN/MINERAL ANALYSIS PER POUND.

Vitamin A	.....	1875 I.U.
Vitamin D	.....	500 I.U.
Vitamin E	.....	20 I.U.
Choline	.....	400 mg.
Folacin	.....	300 mg.
Niacin	.....	14 mg.
Pantothenic Acid	.....	5.75 mg.
Riboflavin	.....	3 mg.
Vitamin B6	.....	1.5 mg.
Thiamin	.....	1 mg.
Vitamin B12	.....	15 mcg.
Vitamin K	.....	.5 mg
Biotin	.....	.04 mg.
Calcium	.....	.80%
Phosphorus	.....	.70%
Potassium	.....	.28%
Sodium	.....	.09%
Magnesium	.....	.04%
Zinc	.....	85 mg.
Iron	.....	80 mg.
Manganese	.....	36 mg.
Copper	.....	5 mg.
Iodine	.....	1 mg.
Selenium	.....	1 mg.

How to order other books by this author   August 1993

If these items are not available in your local bookstores, you may purchase directly from the publisher. Mail you order with your check or purchase order to: Jordan Valley Heritage House, 43592 Hwy. 226, Stayton, Oregon 97383

Books by Colene Copeland. For ages 6 thru 11.
The PRISCILLA Series.

Priscilla (hc)	$9.95 plus $1.25 p&h per copy
Priscilla (pb)	$3.95 plus $1.00 p&h per copy
Little Prissy and T.C. (hc)	$9.95 plus $1.25 p&h per copy
Little Prissy and T.C. (pb)	$4.95 plus $1.00 p&h per copy
Piston and the Porkers (hc)	$9.95 plus $1.25 p&h per copy
Piston and the Porkers (pb)	$4.95 plus $1.00 p&h per copy
Mystery in the Farrowing Barn (hc)	$9.95 plus $1.25 p&h per copy
Mystery in the Farrowing Barn (pb)	$4.95 plus $1.00 p&h per copy
Wanted: Pot Bellied Pigs (hc)	$9.95 plus $1.25 p&h per copy
Wanted: Pot Bellied Pigs (pb)	$4.95 plus $1.00 p&h per copy

Priscilla Presentation -- Video tape (VHS or Beta) This is the author at school, telling her side of the Priscilla story, what it was really like raising a pig in the house. Kids love this hilarious tale!

$29.95 postage paid
rental -- $5.00 postage paid

Youth book by Christina McDade
(ages 10-16)

Apples in the Sky (pb) $3.95 plus $1.00 p&h per copy

Thank you   Postage credit issued